Buying You

By

Wendy Rathbone

**Buying You Copyright © 2018
by Wendy Rathbone and Eye Scry Publications**

Cover design: Sadie Sins

**A publication by:
Eye Scry Publications**
http://www.eyescrypublications.com

ISBN # 978-1-942415-22-0
TITLE: Buying You
Author: Wendy Rathbone

Address all inquiries to the author at:
wrathbone@juno.com

Dedicated to:

Della Van Hise

...always and forever...

And much thanks to:

Sadie Sins

*for her gorgeous cover
and brilliant advice*

*

Christina E. Pilz

*for beta-reading,
Sunday chats
and invaluable encouragement*

Part One

♦

The Date

*

Chapter One

The sign said: *Fantasy Dates, Auction:* **4 p.m.** *For Charity*.

A nervous tremor rippled through Dane's body, and he let out a low laugh at his apprehension. Stupid, really, to be afraid of a crowd. He'd been the star of drama class in high school, but he still suffered from stage fright. Now, though he was known for some of his higher profile modeling ads, he never performed for a crowd at his job. Not a real crowd. The onlookers he was used to were camera guys, make up artists, set designers, fashion consultants. The public only saw him after the fact, touched up, stretched, tanned, air-brushed and enhanced in still photos on billboards, posters and magazines.

Now they would all be looking at him. *Him.* Not to mention, this was his boyhood town. There might be people at the auction he knew. It should have made it easier to think about, but instead it made him feel hyper, unsure.

But just a date with the winner, one night on the town, that seemed harmless enough. One date. Nothing more. The money he and the others would bring in was going to a worthy cause. Helping to fund a local homeless shelter.

He'd agreed to this not because he cared that much about good PR, but mainly because this was his hometown. It was always good to remember, when he was hobnobbing in L.A. or NYC with people who seemed displaced from the struggles of everyday reality, that he came from a small community and a mid-class tract house where people had barbeques and birthday parties in their backyards on Saturdays.

He did not want to come back here to live, no, but he did feel pangs of nostalgia every once in a while. His parents had divorced when he was thirteen, and both had since moved to different cities, but this place was less than an hour from L.A. and this visit for the charity auction sounded fun.

Dane had already resigned himself to a date with a woman, maybe even a minor politician in the town, or a restaurant owner, or a real estate broker. They would be the ones to afford him.

Though he was gay, he didn't mention it to the organizing committee when he'd said yes. This was for raising money, not his pleasure. He'd have dinner with the woman who bought him and that would be that. It wasn't like he hadn't dated women before he finally came to terms with himself that he was gay. So no, he didn't mind going out with a woman. He might even kiss her good night. It wasn't a hardship.

But still. His apprehension returned.

Dane rounded the community center auditorium, a square, stucco structure, found the entrance and pulled open one of two glass doors. When he was little, he used to come here for Halloween carnivals. Over the years, the building had changed very little.

He entered a brightly lit foyer. The gray floor tile shone from recent waxing. He heard voices up ahead. Past the foyer, the tile gave way to a line of blue carpet that led around a white wall to a long lobby, and there he saw posters on A-frames advertising the auction, and the list of names of the people who'd volunteered to be "fantasy dates." Between the posters sat a table covered with red cloth. White hearts with ribbons attached to them lay on the table. Two women sat behind it.

Dane approached.

"Ah, our star of the night," one said.

"Dane Asher." The second one picked up a white heart and held it out to him, a ribbon necklace attached. "Welcome! This is so exciting. Put this on around your neck. Then find your way up to the stage. We have chairs there. Some of our dates have already arrived. You'll see them."

They both looked him up and down, grinning.

He'd dressed in his nicest suit, black with a fuchsia tie and matching fuchsia handkerchief. He wasn't as perfect as his pictures, but he knew he looked good. He took the heart and placed the ribbon necklace over his head.

The first woman said, "Thank you so much for coming. Our charity will benefit greatly. I know you'll take the highest bid."

"Thank you," he said, giving her a grin, happy to see her blush.

He moved past the table to the first set of doors to the auditorium. Instantly, the air became drier, cooler and serene. It was always like that entering a theatre, as if the huge expanse of it was designed in such a way as to quicken the senses. Hushed voices came from all over. Some people had already come in to take their seats.

The stage, golden-lit, had a fairly rudimentary set up. A line of folding chairs, a podium, some pretty, potted mini-trees to each side of the stage to add a little greenery.

Dane moved down the carpeted aisle. The lights were on, but dim. The corners of the auditorium held shadows that gave the place a bigger feel, more magnificent than it really was.

As he passed by some audience members, their heads turned, trying to place him. He gave them his best *I'm charmed* smile and headed to the side of the stage and the steps.

Over half the chairs on the stage were already occupied. He recognized one character actor from an old TV series, the owner of a large car lot off the interstate who always did his own commercials, and a female comedian he'd seen once on Netflix. The rest were mysteries. Most were young, but not all. The car salesman was a rugged, handsome forty-something. A couple of others looked to be in that age range as well.

Ever polite, Dane shook hands with each person on the stage and took a seat at the end of the line-up.

As he waited for the event to start, Dane tried not to fidget. The chair back pressed cold into his back. The seat was hard. His knee bounced. He stretched his leg out to keep himself still. There was no reason for him to be nervous as this was all fun. But his skin felt clammy, cool and hot at the same time.

He was definitely not the performer-type when it came to playing himself. Give him a character, a script, and once he got past the stage fright, he was fine. Let people take their pictures and do whatever they wanted to his body on film, but in real life, he preferred his privacy. Luckily, the chairs on the stage filled up quickly as more and more audience filed in, the noise level rising, people laughing, some pointing or staring at the people on the stage. Dane rested his hands on the tops of his thighs, focusing on keeping his fingers from curling into fists. He didn't have to wait long before the auction began.

First, the two women who'd greeted people in the lobby came on stage. Each gave short speeches about how happy they were to have this event, thanking the volunteers, and all the contestants on the stage.

They talked about their charity and all the various events they were doing to raise money for it. Dane listened but wasn't sure his brain absorbed most of it. He kept his hands clasped tightly in front of him.

Next, the auctioneer came out, an older man with a voice perfectly toned for selling. He introduced himself as "Bill" and quickly gave a run-down on the auction rules. Dane stared straight ahead, the flutter in his stomach making him wish for it all to be quickly over.

Finally, the auction began.

People loved the way Bill made jokes. He described the dates as "items" and pushed for higher bids. The audience made lots of noise, rooting for the person being auctioned off, encouraging bidders to go higher. The audience had little heart-shaped paddles they waved to bid.

Dane felt himself grinning as he watched. He did not realize until about half-way through the line-up of contestants that he was probably being saved for last. The best for last? He hated to think it, but as a model he was used to being bought for his looks. His appearance was what paid his bills, and it would hopefully pay a lot into this particular charity as well.

But as the time got closer to his turn, his heart sped up. The nervousness made him feel like he had back in his school days. He'd been the best-looking kid in class, even starring in school plays, but still insecure. After his parents divorced, he'd been angry and hurt, and he'd spent a couple of difficult teen years being haughty and rude, pushing people away, having a hard time making friends. Later, in high school, he'd become somewhat popular, even being voted in the class yearbook "guy most likely to break everyone's heart" but it was because he was tall and dark, lean and blue-eyed. He could grab attention with his smile. But none of it really meant anything. And none of his friends were ever close friends. He'd kept in touch with no one from that era.

That withdrawn feeling had lifted somewhat when he'd begun to get modeling jobs, but he still held back from relationships. He'd dated only two women early on, which led to nothing. He'd had three short hook ups his entire life, all with men. One of the hook-ups had led to a brief dating stint that ended badly. He didn't think too much about that. He was still young. He had his entire life ahead of him.

"And now we arrive at our final offering," said Bill proudly. "I'm sure you've all been waiting to bid on this one! Dane Asher!"

When he heard his name called, it came to him as if through an echoing tunnel. He rose gracefully from his chair to the sound of clapping and cheers. He automatically donned his perfect smile, and came to stand beside the podium, raising his hands modestly and shaking his head. When he stood next to Bill, the applause growing louder, the butterflies became a frenzy in his stomach.

In truth, he felt good-natured about it all. It was only nerves that made him wish he was anywhere but here.

"You may have seen Dane in the famous Tokatu underwear ads."

Dane's face flushed when he turned his head and saw, on the huge TV behind him, his image come up for all to view. The ad they had chosen to showcase him and remind the audience of who they were bidding for was one of his most recent, and most famous.

In the photo, he lounged in a red velvet chair, one leg up on the chair's armrest, the other draped over the seat. His dark bangs spread in artful spikes across his forehead, and the waves of the rest of his hair were slicked back, behind his ears. His eyes appeared almost cat-like, the blue enhanced of course, as if his irises were made of sapphire.

His pose showed off his sculpted chest and arms, bare and tanned, to full effect. His crotch was nicely rounded in the white briefs, promising a package worth unwrapping. The ad communicated that you, too, could have a promising package and look like this if you were to buy this underwear with this label and wear it everywhere you went.

Dane was proud of the ad—he looked good--but standing live in front of an audience, that familiar stage fright always threatened just beneath the surface. His face grew hot as he heard the whoops and catcalls from the audience.

"Dane Asher is single, twenty-four, six foot three, and well on his way to becoming a super-model, and we are so happy he took time out of his busy schedule to be here for our charity. So bid. Bid high. Bid often." Laughter from the audience. "Oh, and did I forget to add? Bid high!"

Bill sold him like a pro. His voice rang over the auditorium with a tone and resonance that encouraged and enticed without sounding like he was begging. He'd done a fine job so far of raising money and getting high bids for all the contestants.

Dane forced a smile, willing himself to relax. He took a deep breath, which helped. Soon the bidding began.

Dane could not keep track of all the bids flying about. He only knew that the auctioneer was talking rapidly, repeating shouted numbers, pressing for more bids, and that the audience responded with equal enthusiasm.

When he heard the number "nine hundred" he had the brief thought, *Will the bidding go to four figures?* No contestant had been bid that high. Only one had made it to past eight hundred. This was not a rich town. It was already taking them forever to raise the money for the shelter.

Suddenly, a voice called out from the back of the auditorium.

"Four thousand!"

A hush spread over the crowd.

All the bids so far had come from women.

The voice came from a figure wearing a dark blue hoodie. And it was male.

10

The auctioneer turned to Dane, leaning away from the microphone. "Are you okay with this bid?"

"Yes. I made no specifications as to the gender of my date." But now his interest peaked. The idea that a man might buy his time for the evening had not occurred to him. Of course, he liked it.

Since he was not publicly "out" the auctioneer made a polite comment about the situation.

"In the code of good sportsmanship, Mr. Asher has given his go-ahead that a bidder of any gender is acceptable."

The audience erupted in loud applause and whistles.

Dane squinted toward the back of the room, trying to see the man better. But the sweatshirt hood put his face in shadow. All Dane could make out was a lean build in what might be black jeans. The hands were hidden in the hoodie's pockets. He looked tall, but not as tall as Dane.

"Four thousand has been bid. Do I hear four thousand fifty?"

Silence met the auctioneer's voice. Dane glanced about, the lights of the stage casting the audience into silhouettes, the air stirred by occasional dust motes.

It seemed to take forever for Bill to pound his gavel to end the game.

When the bang came, Dane jolted, but kept smiling, hoping no one noticed how nervous he still was.

"Sold! A date for the evening with Mr. Dane Asher for four thousand dollars, and our record bid for the evening! Thank you, Mr. Asher, for your participation in tonight's charity event."

Dane waved to the audience and walked off-stage to the table where the bidders came to pay for their purchases.

Chapter Two

As he stood waiting for his bidder to show, Dane scanned the crowd. People were standing, walking up and down the aisles, some leaving, some just hanging out. He could not see the man in the hoodie.

After about five minutes, a young man in a black suit approached the table. In his hand he had two envelopes. He handed one to the cashier, and one to Dane.

He said quietly, "Payment. And a note for you, sir."

"Are you who bid on me?"

"No, sir. I am the chauffeur."

"Chauffeur?"

"Read the note, sir."

Dane opened the envelope. The texture of the paper against his fingertips felt soft, expensive. The creamy coloring added to its formality. He slid out a thin, single sheet of paper, folded in thirds.

He unfolded it and read the neatly, hand-printed note:

Mr. Asher:

The limo is for you. The driver is instructed to take you to my home, about a twenty minute journey from where you now stand.

Help yourself to the champagne from the fridge in the back seat.

Dinner will be served at 7.

I look forward to meeting you.

K.

Dane looked up from the short letter to the limo driver.

"He already left?" Dane asked.

"Yes, sir. He said he had some things to attend to, but will be awaiting your arrival."

"He didn't even give his name in this note. Who is he?"

"You will have to ask him that question, sir," The driver looked too young to sound so formal.

"You don't even know his name?"

"I was instructed not to say. I drive for his company, sir. I go where he tells me to go. I was instructed to come here and pick you up. He told me to tell you to call him K."

"Then he already knew he was going to win me."

"Yes, sir. He seemed very sure of that."

Bill came over to them. "Is there a problem? Are you having second thoughts, Mr. Asher?"

"No, no. I'm fine. I just expected to meet my date here and leave together. But now he's sent a limo and… and I have my car here."

"That is not a problem, sir," the limo driver said. "He told me to tell you not to worry about your car. When the date is over, you will be brought back here."

"Are you all right with that?" asked Bill.

"Yes. Yes. It's fine. I just wondered who he is." Dane leaned toward the cashier. "Did he pay with a check? Does it have a name?"

The woman holding the check looked closer at it. "It's a company check, from something called Trans Corp. I can't make out the signature, just a K for the first part and maybe that's a P or an N in the last name? I don't know. It's mostly a squiggle."

"So you're okay to go?" Bill asked. "Because we want everyone to be happy tonight. No sour notes. It's all fun, right?"

"Right," Dane replied. "It's fine. The note says dinner will be served at his home."

"If you don't want to go to a stranger's home—"

"No, no. It's fine."

"Just to be on the safe side," the auctioneer said to the driver, "will you supply us with the address? We don't want any funny business, of course."

"Of course." The driver took a pen from an inside pocket of his suit jacket and wrote the address on the envelope that had held the check.

"All right, then," the driver said, handing the envelope over. "Shall we go then, Mr. Asher?"

Dane forced a grin, showing them all how good-natured he could be. "Lead the way."

*

Dane followed the limo driver outside and down the concrete path to the parking lot.

The auction had begun at four o'clock and it was now six. It was a Sunday in early fall and the sun had just begun to set. Pink stretched toward the western horizon, disrupting the usual ashy haze of smog. The air smelled clean, tinged with the breath of a cool breeze. Dane smelled roses blooming along the edge of the building, and the cut grass of a nearby field where children were finishing a late afternoon game of soccer.

The limo purred in the red zone at the end of the cement walkway right in front of the theatre building, as if limos and the very rich did not have to care about rules or laws or petty parking tickets.

The driver held the back door open for Dane, who could already see the plush leather seats curving along the front and sides within, and the long table with holders for bottles and glasses. The table was already set up. On one holder a bottle of champagne glittered from a silver bucket of ice. Beside the bucket sat a fluted, crystal glass.

Dane got in and sat closest to the front along one side, feeling how the leather cushioned his body. Windows ran along both sides and above his head a moon roof with squares of glass like latticework showed him the pre-night sky. Gold lights ran in pretty lines along the tops of the windows. It all smelled like leather and soap, and seemed like it might be ready to take off to the stars.

"Make yourself comfortable, sir," said the driver.

Dane poured himself a glass of champagne and sat back to watch the scenery pass by as the streetlights came on and the sun dipped below the skyline.

The champagne tasted faintly sweet. The crystal glass Dane drank from felt thin and fragile in his hand.

They headed east on the freeway for about ten minutes before exiting. Dane saw hills darkening in shadow, and houselights far above.

The road curved and turned into a lane. They passed grassy banks and sycamore, willow, eucalyptus and old oaks with the leaves falling in shadows. Between the trees were gated driveways and Dane could see fancy houses set back from the road, far enough apart from each other for privacy but still close enough to be a neighborhood. A very posh neighborhood.

After a while, when Dane thought for sure they would run out of hill or road, the limo turned onto one of the gated driveways, stopping for a moment and idling.

The gate was black iron with a dragonfly design that broke down the center as it swung open. To the sides in front, thick overgrowths of ivy and bougainvillea climbed a matching iron fence. Through that foliage, Dane could make out a little of the interior grounds lit by lamps on tall posts all the way up the drive. A lot of lawn and more trees spread up toward the house.

As the limo began to move again, the grounds came into view. He turned his head to look out both sides to see trellises, a large gazebo, and a lit-up patio closer to the house that provided an awning for a waterfall pouring into a large swimming pool.

15

Who was this guy who'd bought him? And why all the mystery? Could it be someone from the fashion industry who knew him? Someone rich and mysterious who'd had their eye on him?

In truth, life did not work out that way. He'd talked to enough bitter models to understand reality. Models were a dime a dozen, tossed out as "old" before they knew what hit them. They were the types the wealthy courted for temporary liaisons, if that. The people who ran the fashion world were the foundation of it, of course, and the models were the decorations that got changed yearly due to what was trending in the moment.

Dane was trending at the moment. He hoped for a super-model career that might last into his thirties, but so did everyone else. He did not like to think he'd be past his prime by this time next year, but he had been saving his paychecks just in case and not jet-setting about the world, or buying expensive cars and houses.

The driveway led to a circle paved with rock. Pink flagstones. At the center of the circle a fountain shaped like a giant bird sprayed water and mist into the air. The front porch, rather small for such a large structure, stood tall, the double doors consisting of stained glass patterned with dragonflies about eight feet in height.

The limo stopped at the curb, which curved to form a low, short path to the front steps.

Over hidden speakers in the limo, the driver's voice announced, "We have arrived at our destination."

Dane watched the driver get out and walk around the car to open the doors for him. He put his glass down.

"You may take your champagne with you if you'd like."

Dane shook his head, climbing empty-handed out of the back.

"This place is huge."

"Yes, sir."

"And gorgeous."

"Yes, sir."

Dane looked up. Two stories of bright gold windows, high, peaked roofs, and white paint met his gaze. He could not tell exactly how big the house was, but the front was wide and he could sense that the rest of the house stretched far back onto the property.

Overhead, the sky had become swirls of silver, purple and pale pink. From his vantage on the first step of the porch, the view sprawled in a spectacular array of scattered lights of various cities as far as the eye could see. The sun had set and the skyline was a vivid, electric orange.

Even though it was California, land of one season, he could still smell autumn in the air. There was a hint of chimney smoke, and the breeze had a distant salt edge.

"You can go up now, sir. The butler will let you in."

The driver leaned against the side of the limo, arms crossed, white gloves pressing his chest. He nodded with a half-smile.

Dane turned and went up the steps. Just as he came to the wider expanse of the porch, the double doors opened, glass dragonflies flashing in the last of the waning daylight.

A man in a tuxedo, with gray and brown hair and a short gray beard, bowed and motioned him in. "Welcome," he said. "My name is Ben. May I take your jacket?"

Dane had felt warm since the auction. All the excitement of it, the newness of his surroundings, and not knowing what to expect, plus one glass of champagne had done little to cool him off.

He nodded, and gave his suit jacket over to Ben, feeling freer now in his white shirt and trim vest.

"Who is my host for tonight?" he asked.

"He will be joining you shortly in the dining hall. I will take you there now."

Dane breathed in the deep sweetness of candles on the air. He looked around at the huge foyer. Several white rugs on a shining marble floor led to a deeper interior. A large ornate mirror over a mahogany wall table reflected the room into itself, giving even more depth. Orchids stood in a vase on the table, the pale lavender blooms tilted as if to gaze into the mirror.

Art hung on the walls, abstract and modern with a palette of blended colors: blue, purple, dark green. The paintings looked like strange storms captured and held upon their windows of canvas.

"This way, sir," said Ben.

As they came out of the foyer, they rounded a corner and entered a large area, almost like a waiting room. Twin staircases curved opposite each other, their banisters gleaming. On either side of the ground floor, short halls led to closed doors.

One door stood open to the right. Dane could see it was a dining room with a long table covered with a red cloth and sporting a tall candelabrum at its center. Five tall white candles glowed in its holders.

The butler ushered him through the wide entryway. "Sir, may I get you a drink? Anything you like."

Dane wasn't a big drinker like some on the social scenes he traveled, but he did like wine better than champagne. Though the champagne in the limo had been top of the line.

"Wine? Sauvignon Blanc?" Dane asked.

"Yes, sir."

Dane stood in the huge dining room while Ben went to a bar and poured the drink.

The dining table was long enough to seat twelve. Only two places were set, one at each end, all formal and distant-looking. The napkins were white cloth and had been folded into fans sitting on the plates. The silverware was not silver but gold. And crystal water glasses sat full and misted with condensation as if they had been recently poured.

Dane pulled out his cell phone to note the time. 6:45. The note had said dinner would be at seven. He turned to Ben.

"I'm early."

"Yes. You may sit if you like," Ben said.

"I think I'd like to look around this room."

"Of course, sir. I can bring appetizers if you'd like."

"No, thank you."

Though he ran three to four miles almost every day, and worked with weights three days a week, he still liked to stay away from things called *appetizers*. He needed to be lean-muscled for his job. That meant, for him, lots of greens, protein, a bite of bread here and there, and rarely fried foods or desserts. But tonight he figured he could indulge a little. Thus the champagne. And the wine.

He'd also fasted since breakfast, deciding he would eat what was served to him. He'd expected the "date" to be at a restaurant, though. And he'd expected a female. In fact, he'd hoped for a female because then he would not feel anything, and he would not have to wonder what it might be like if the date progressed because he would not allow that to happen with a woman.

Apprehension coursed through his body, making his muscles tense. His veins had an inner burn. He moved toward the wall to look at the paintings and distract himself.

More abstracts. Slashes of vermillion, purple, pink. He looked without really seeing down the line of paintings – three in all, tastefully spread across a clean white wall—and his thoughts churned.

He could not quite get over it yet. A man had bought him for the evening. For charity, of course, but still... It was a man. A rich man by the look of it. Someone who had bid four thousand dollars, more than anyone else had bid the entire evening. Someone who had provided a limo, champagne, and a regal butler with wine.

Sighing, he turned toward the table. He looked closer at the candelabrum, the centerpiece of the dining table, and saw it was dark copper sculpted into nude figures holding their hands above their heads. The candles glimmered but the real light came from a chandelier overhead that looked like rain caught and suspended in one section of the ceiling. The fall of liquid light spread throughout the room giving it a silvery glow.

Everywhere he looked, things glittered. The glasses, the cutlery, the plates. The silver band on his middle finger.

Ben spoke from behind him, nearly startling him.

"Your date will be here in a few minutes. Would you like to wash up? The door at your far right leads to a washroom."

"Thank you." Grateful for something else to distract himself, Dane went into the bathroom. When he put his hands in the sink, the faucet came on as it sensed his hands moving underneath. The towels were soft and dark purple. The air smelled like a meadow. The rug under his shoes felt like he was walking on pillows.

Glancing into the mirror, he straightened his hair, brushing aside a few errant bangs, running his fingers through the waves at his neck. Everything was right. He was ready.

Chapter Three

Dane stepped into the dining room. His body was hot but his hands felt cold. Ben stood by the wide entrance looking out toward the twin staircases as Dane came up alongside him.

A door slammed shut.

Dane realized he was holding his breath. Silly. This was a date for charity. Nothing more. So what if the guy was mysterious and rich?

He heard a voice, tone low and echoing like a hum, the words coming fast. A man was talking on a cell.

Ben straightened, white-gloved hands behind his back.

Dane peered around his shoulder.

It was not the man in the hoodie he now saw. Or, if it was that man, he had changed clothes. This guy wore a grey suit with no tie, his white shirt unbuttoned at the throat. He was slim, not quite as broad-shouldered as Dane, nor as tall. He had glints of blond throughout his light brown hair which he wore loose and straight over the ears, neatly trimmed, with the bangs combed back to reveal a smooth, wide forehead.

The man was handsome, there could be no doubt, but more than that, he exuded an energy that seemed to spark the air about him as he came forward, hissing "Later!" into the phone and then slamming it down on the butler's tray.

He did not even glance at Dane. Instead, he looked at Ben and said, "Take that phone out of here, please. I want no interruptions during dinner!"

"Yes, sir."

The man turned toward the dining table. "No appetizers for my guest?"

"He did not want them, sir."

"Oh, all right." The man seemed perturbed. "Bring the food then. And take my jacket." He shrugged out of his coat.

Ben held out his free hand, taking the garment over his free arm, then disappeared to another room.

Dane watched the fiery young man walk about the table as if inspecting it for flaws. Something about him was familiar, but Dane couldn't place it.

He liked the way the guy moved, and more, he was Dane's type. Fairer than Dane, light green eyes, smaller build but still filling out his clothing.

Dane liked the energy. He liked wiry and enthusiastic men over the darker broody types. He liked when he saw vitality in their eyes. Liveliness. This was a type that would have caught Dane's eye in a crowd, would have made him curious, interested. Enticed. It had happened to him only a couple of times in his life, this type of attraction, that sudden feeling of not just deliciousness, but "I want to know you."

So far, the man had not introduced himself. Had not even looked at him. Dane knew rudeness among the wealthy was not rare. It was an affected smugness of privilege. That still didn't make it right.

Dane crossed his arms in front of his chest, shaking off the nerves for a moment. "Are you the one who bid on me and won?" He still wasn't sure.

The man looked up briefly, as if he'd just noticed that Dane was in the room. His eyebrows were raised, his look almost innocent. "I am. Are you surprised?"

Dane wanted to hold out his hand, as was proper in introductions, but the man was too far away.

"Well, yes, actually. And hello. My name is Dane." He realized only after he'd said it that the man already knew his name.

"Yes, I know." He sounded as if his mind was on other things. As if this date was almost an annoyance.

Dane said, "Well, I want to thank you for the nice limo ride. And your house is beautiful. I didn't expect a mere date to become-- this."

The man sounded as if he actually snorted as he made his way about the table, fingers running around the smooth edge.

"You don't expect everything to always go your way?" asked he man. "You? A successful model?"

That put Dane on the spot for a moment. He did not know how to respond.

"I don't—"

"You've probably been spoiled a lot."

And this man hadn't? Dane swallowed, glancing about the ornate and luxurious room.

Again, Dane had the feeling that he'd seen this guy before. He couldn't place it.

The man's hand rose as if to smack the air. "You know, with your looks, your successes, you always get whatever you want."

Still, this guy—this man who was so totally his type—had not told him his name. Would not look at him.

"You might be thinking I have whatever I want, too. And yes, I have this house, and my phone does not stop ringing. But it wasn't like this until a few years ago. I wasn't raised here. My phone didn't always ring."

His host was making a lot of assumptions, almost as if he resented Dane.

"Well, anyway." He pivoted to finally face Dane, standing some distance away, head bowed in such a way as to keep him not quite in focus. "Four thousand dollars for a date. I'm wondering, what might I expect for that sum?"

Dane cleared his throat. "Dinner, I guess."

"You don't sound sure."

"I am sure." Dane forced a smile, one of his charmer grins. "I expected a date, a date for charity, to include dinner. Yes. Of course."

"Of course."

What other plans might this intriguing guy have? Dane didn't want to speculate. He didn't quite trust the situation.

And he didn't want to think any further than the table, and eating.

"Well, dinner it will be. Care to have a seat?" The man gestured to the end of the table nearest to where Dane stood.

"But," said Dane, going for a casual tone despite the strangeness of the scene. "How can I have dinner with you if I don't know your name?"

He saw a sharp eyebrow rise. A moment of disappointed confusion crossed the fine features. "You don't know me. Of course you don't-- Call me Kai."

Okay, Dane thought. *Not K. Or Kay. But Kai. Rhyming with buy.* "Nice to meet you, Kai."

Kai did not smile. "I'm sure the feeling is mutual."

Dane heard the double meaning behind the words and didn't like it at all. He had the sudden thought he was being duped. Maybe hidden cameras were rolling. Maybe it was all a big joke for reasons he could not fathom. His first impression of this guy was that he was Dane's type. Now he was re-thinking everything.

Dane sat first, reluctant now, untrusting. The man was so far away it felt like they were separated by barriers of time itself. Again, he thought it all might be some trick. Or maybe he was dreaming.

Kai moved to his own chair, sitting with graceful ease, and picked up his spoon.

Immediately Ben came in followed by two servants, one male, one female, dressed in black trousers and white shirts and bow ties. The servants placed bowls of soup on the plates before Kai and Dane. Steam rose from their depths.

Vegetable soup. Thin. Dark brown.

Ben re-filled Dane's glass of wine.

He then filled Kai's glass from another wine bottle. Red.

Kai lifted his glass. "Here's to charity."

Dane lifted his glass. "To charity."

Kai lifted his spoon and took a mouthful of soup.

Dane did the same. It was excellent. And he realized despite his nerves, he was quite hungry.

"I'm sure you have all sorts of funny modeling stories to tell," Kai said into the silence.

Dane looked up. "Like what?"

"You tell me. It is an interesting line of work, isn't it?"

"It's not all glamour if that's what you're thinking."

"What then?" Kai asked.

"Tedious hours of photo shoots. Getting every detail perfect only to have it photo-shopped out of the final cut. Starving myself for a day before every shoot."

"You starve yourself?"

"Haven't you heard of suffering for art?" Dane asked.

"Hmm, that doesn't sound like much fun."

"The paychecks are worth it."

"I would guess the notoriety is nice," said Kai, though he didn't sound as if he really meant it. "You get invited to posh parties. You get to have your choice of companions for the evening. The partying probably gets downright rowdy."

Dane blinked at him over the fluttering candlelight. "You don't have it so bad. You seem quite successful yourself."

Kai gave a short laugh. "This old place? Yeah, it's nice, isn't it?"

"What do you do?"

"I own an app company. Weather apps got us started and still take in the biggest royalties. In college, well, this classmate and I—we started it. It took off. It's a boring story. But you—not so boring. Modeling. Starving. Sounds far more exciting. Do you do runway modeling, too?"

"I haven't yet."

"Did you still have to learn to walk and turn and all that sort of thing?"

"No. But the shoots are always quite a production and there is a lot of drama."

"Would you prefer the runway?"

"No. I like the photo shoots just fine."

"Ah, you can distance yourself then. You don't have to play to a crowd. But why not? You definitely have the ability. Like acting. You're into it. You played the crowd quite nicely at the auction this evening."

How could Kai know that Dane had been into acting? A lucky guess?

Dane finished his soup and put down his spoon. As soon as he did so, a servant took the plate and the soup bowl away.

Dane said, "I don't remember playing the crowd. I just stood there."

Had he done anything? He couldn't remember. And now he was second-guessing himself which he had stopped doing years ago. Being on stage was like that for him in high school. Often he would walk out in front of an audience and go into a sort of blank haze. All he could think to do was keep his head up, eyes open. Eventually the lines he'd memorized came to him and he forgot himself in the role. He always finished his performance anxious that he'd done something wrong. But everyone had always loved him. He'd worried for nothing.

"I suppose, for you, just standing there is playing the crowd," said Kai.

Dane watched a servant take away Kai's plate and bowl. Ben stood by the door overlooking it all as if he were waiting for the servers to make a mistake.

"I'm not sure what you mean by that," Dane said.

Kai glanced to the side, eyes catching the light, and for a moment they turned gold. He gave a half-hearted laugh. "Take the compliment for what it is."

Biting the inside of his cheek, Dane fidgeted, letting Kai fade in his vision. The man exuded a lustrous handsome aura. Why was he talking this way, coldly grilling him?

Despite the strange attraction Dane felt toward Kai, their conversation was out of step, timed wrong, hollow. As if they were really talking about something else between the words, only Dane could not hear what was being said. Something more was going on under the surface of things. He just didn't know what yet.

A servant brought the next course. A green salad with carrot shavings, purple cabbage, cherry tomatoes and vinaigrette on the side. It was laid out on a gold-edged plate as though it had been designed by an artist.

Dane took a sip of wine. He stared at the salad. He had nothing against salads but this had to be the millionth one he'd had in a year. He was tired of them.

He picked up his fork in his left hand and poured some of the dressing onto the salad with his right. He took a bite. It was too sweet. He put his fork down.

He looked up to see Kai staring at him.

"Don't like salads?"

"I love them."

"I can see that."

More hollow banter. And something almost like bitterness in the air between them.

"You look familiar to me," Dane said suddenly.

"Really?" Now Kai leaned forward. He wasn't eating the salad, either.

Dane shook his head. "We haven't met before, have we?"

"I should think if we had you'd remember."

Dane blinked rapidly. Kai had phrased that sentence in such a way as to remain vague and give a faint hint that he knew more than he was letting on.

"I'm trying to figure out why you look familiar," said Dane, trying to remain polite about it when Kai seemed to be playing games with him.

Kai made a gesture to Ben. The servants came and took away their uneaten salads. Well, at least they had that in common. Neither was in the mood for fresh greens at the moment.

"Do I look familiar to you?" Dane asked.

"Oh, well, I've seen your underwear ads. So of course your—uh—face is familiar to me." He let out a laugh that died too quickly.

"Yes, well, I get that a lot. People think they know me but don't remember from where. But then it's there right in front of them on billboards, magazine covers, taxi cabs, buses, trains."

"Of course. You're everywhere."

The servants brought the main course, what looked like small, baked chickens, seasoned red potatoes, and green string beans with mushrooms. What a relief there was nothing fried, and yet right now Dane could have eaten a large order of steak fries with a side of ranch dressing for dipping. That was what happened when he felt nervous or out of his league. He reached for the junk food.

When he was a kid, it was his temper he'd had to learn to deal with, and more so after his parents divorced. He got hot and furious fast, especially if he was embarrassed. He learned to look away from situations that made him uncomfortable, to walk away.

Now he took a deep breath, unwilling to walk away. "That doesn't explain why you're familiar to me."

Kai tilted his head, picked up a knife and fork, and started cutting on his chicken.

"Ah, that is the crux of it. It doesn't explain it at all," Kai said.

When no more of an explanation was forthcoming, Dane focused on his food. The servants brought warm bread and soft, creamy butter. He thought he could afford one bite but did not reach for a slice. The yearning for carbs when he was tense was a dangerous one. He could all too easily over-indulge.

For several minutes they ate in silence. Dane eyed the warm bread but did not touch it. They each had their own basket.

Finally, Kai broke the silence. "The bread's fresh-made from the kitchen. Tonight is not the night to starve yourself."

It was kindest thing Kai had said so far.

Dane allowed a smile to curve his lips and reached for a slice hidden among soft linens in his small, dark basket, and at the same time Kai reached for a slice.

"Melts in your mouth," Kai said, as he bit into the bread.

Dane had not, for one moment, thought otherwise. Just the scent alone of doughy yeast still steaming made his mouth water. That, and his lovely date if he weren't so defensive and standoffish.

Dane spread a thin layer of butter across the bread and took a bite. The flavor washed over his entire body. He barely chewed before it dissolved down his throat.

"Good?"

"Very." He took another bite, loving not only the taste but the texture.

As he ate the rest of the fine meal, his mind kept trying to figure out why he found Kai so familiar. And why Kai was, in fact, being quite defensive. Even resentful. Kai was the one who'd paid for the evening. If he didn't want Dane here, then why?

"So, did you always want to be a model?" Kai asked.

Surprised at the question, Dane said, "No. I fell into it, actually. I wanted to act."

"Oh? Well, it couldn't have been easy. So many contenders. Just finding an agent is hard, I hear. Did you know someone?"

Dane nodded. "A friend of a friend. And I got lucky."

"Seems luck favors men like you."

"And you?" Dane asked. "You have a successful company. And you—uh—well, you are good looking."

"You think so?" Kai did not look up.

Dane nodded, chewing.

"Your description page for the evening, for the auction and the date. It didn't state that you're gay," Kai said.

"No." Even though Dane had just said Kai was handsome, it still startled him that Kai knew this fact about him, as if Kai had researched him beforehand, and not deduced Dane's identity in the moment.

"Why not?" Kai asked.

"I didn't want to bring attention in that way, over-complicate things."

"Plus, you're not out publicly. I looked. Online."

"You did?"

"Of course. But I still attended the auction. I still bid. Why do you think I bid on you, then?"

"I don't know." More discomfort. Dane wanted another slice of bread. Badly.

"Maybe I could just tell you dated men."

"Could you?" Dane was curious now. Most people could not tell just by looking at him. Even in the industry of fashion where more than half the players were gay, he did not automatically stand out as one of them.

"Or maybe we have mutual friends and I'd just heard it in passing."

That surprised Dane. But then again, maybe not. Kai was rich. Dane sometimes hung out with the rich and famous. The rich often traveled in small circles together.

"Do we?"

"Do we what?" asked Kai.

"Have mutual friends?"

"Wrong again. But you can keep guessing as to why I look familiar. Let's do that over dessert."

"Oh, no dessert for me." Dane waved his hand at his plate. "I'm full." But the mystery still intrigued him.

"It's only fruit. With the sweet cream on the side. And coffee ice cream if you want it."

Dane gave a heavy sigh. He loved sweet cream. This man, who seemed to resent him, was going to go even further and perhaps be his undoing. Not only with dessert, but with a standoffish yet charismatic allure that made Dane want to run away and move closer at the same time. It was interesting to note that someone who did not seem all that forthcoming was perhaps even more enticing for it.

This was so not the date he'd expected this evening.

The fruit dish came. Sliced peaches, strawberries, bananas. All his favorites. He took his spoon and poured a little of the cream on the fruit. How could he resist? This entire night was already over the top. Limos. Mansions. Butlers. And a pretty man who drove him crazy with his weird way of almost despising the date he'd just bought.

Dane took a bite of the dessert and smiled. It was worth it putting up with the guy for this meal. Really worth it.

"So, let's play a game, shall we?" Kai asked.

"What sort of game?" The meal had revived his strength for facing this unusual evening.

"A sort of truth or dare game."

"Sort of?" Dane asked. It was a bit childish, but he was up for it.

"Yes."

"All right then. You start."

Kai smiled, spoon ringing against his dish. "So you are gay, then, am I right?"

"Truth. Yes. My turn."

"Fine," said Kai.

"Are you?" Dane asked.

"Am I what?"

"Gay."

"Truth. Yes," said Kai.

Now that that was established between them, maybe things would get easier. But too soon Dane realized the folly of that thought.

"My turn," Kai said. "Truth or dare. When did you know you were gay?"

Dane wasn't up for dares quite yet.

"Truth. Not until after high school."

"Really?" Kai folded his napkin neatly and placed it on the table. "Are you sure you never had even a hint, a fantasy, a first crush when you were younger than that?"

"I—I—that's two questions." It was obvious Kai was playing the game to hint at why Dane found him so familiar.

"It's the truth part of truth or dare. Just making sure your answers are honest. So, are you sure? Positively sure you had no clue about being gay until after high school?"

"I had some thoughts."

The candlelight was almost hurting his eyes as he looked through it to Kai's still so-familiar face. That dark blond hair, wavy, neatly combed back, glimmered. But that wasn't what spurred the slice of a memory he kept getting. The jaw was narrow but firm, the chin and nose more angular than soft. Was that it? So many people he knew, especially models of both genders had angular features. But, no, his mind was not satisfied. It kept insisting there was a deeper level of recognition. The eyes? The mouth? Before he could focus more on that problem, Kai interrupted.

"So you had some thoughts. Fantasies?" Kai asked.

"Sometimes."

"How young?"

"Very young. As any curious kid might have. My turn," said Dane.

Kai leaned back and crossed his arms.

"Why did you bid on me?" Dane asked.

"Why not?"

"That's not an answer."

"This is a kid's game. It's stupid. Let's do something else." Kai stood and stretched. His arms pulled his white shirt taut against his chest. He wore a thin belt. The silver buckle flashed like a weird code into Dane's eyes.

"I have a beautiful sitting room with a fire going. Will you join me?"

Dane wanted to ask it again. *Why did you buy me?*

Kai picked up his wine glass. "Bring your wine. Ben will pour you more if you need it."

Chapter Four

The date could end now and Dane would have done his duty. A meet and greet and dinner was enough. Wasn't it? What more should he owe to someone—a stranger—who paid four thousand dollars for him? Did Kai expect a lot more? Maybe even adult benefits?

Dane's mind laughed at the idea. He might be a model, but he didn't sell himself that far. Four thousand dollars to charity bought dinner only. A conversation afterward might be too much.

But Dane found he did not yet want the evening to end. He was game for a little more provocation, and his brain would not stop thinking he'd met this attractive guy before.

Dane followed Kai through the hall and out into the front room where the twin staircases curved. A house with two wings—did Kai live here alone? Dane could never understand why people bought such huge homes just because they were rich, unless they had a huge family.

Kai headed toward the wing of the home furthest from the dining room. A short, undecorated hall led to a large, warm room with a hearth nearly as tall as Dane himself, and a huge leather couch as long as two couches if they were pushed end to end.

Glasses of wine and a blazing fire. Both were romantic images.

The couch faced the fireplace where a low table stood in front of it. The floor was marble and reflected the flames from the hearth in coppery, undulating waves. Under the table a plush black rug stretched the length of the couch, huge, wide, and soft underfoot as they came around to sit.

When Dane glanced around the room, he saw broad windows with dark gray floor-to-ceiling curtains, drawn.

Behind them, where the room angled in a sort of "L" shape, he saw a huge flat-screen TV affixed to the white wall and another smaller couch and two recliners facing it.

In a place this huge, Kai could have had a separate TV room. But maybe he liked this room too much to segregate its two functions. Maybe he was as in love with the gigantic hearth as Dane was now that he looked upon its inlaid rocks and crystals on the outside frame that stretched all the way up to the high ceiling. The rocks of the hearth were all colors, sliced through and polished to a dull shine, some pink striped, some turquoise, some quartz. The smallest were the size of Dane's fist; the largest were slabs at least two feet in length shot through with stripes of pink and gold. He decided he could get lost in that hearth for hours.

"The hearth is beautiful."

"Isn't it?" Kai shrugged, not modest in the least. "It was built by the former owner. She was an artist of some repute. She didn't build the home. It's older, been through many owners. But she designed this piece and so it's my favorite room."

Dane nodded. Kai looked to be as young as Dane, so he could not have owned the place for very long. He'd said his company had taken off in college. That couldn't have been more than a couple years ago.

Kai sat at the end of the couch, Dane toward the middle, but it still left many feet between them. Dane wanted to stare at the man until he figured out the puzzle his mind kept posing to him, but refrained. But he kept him in his peripheral vision, and flashed back on the image of Kai walking in front of him.

Kai had sauntered through the place like a guy on a mission, quick in his movements instead of smooth; he was almost jerky. Hyper. There was something about the way the light gleamed against just a few strands of his hair, making it look as if there were thin ribbons of metal threaded at random throughout the locks. And something about the way his shoulders twitched back and his head lifted whenever Dane spoke or moved. Somewhat familiar. Maybe he knew someone with similar mannerisms. That could be it.

Dane said, "So, I know you said the game was stupid, but you still never answered my question."

"Which question was that? I forgot."

"Why did you buy me?"

"Oh, that. Did I pick truth?"

Kai had not picked either truth or dare, but Dane replied, "Yes."

"Does there have to be a reason why I bid on you?"

"By the way you did it, all at the end, yes," Dane said. "You had dinner prepared. You knew you were going to do this. You had this planned."

"Did I?"

"It's obvious."

"Maybe I fell for your billboard ads. Or maybe I just wanted to give a nice sum to charity for a tax write off."

Dane shook his head. He faced the other man. Maybe he could get it out of him that way. "Truth or dare."

"It's my turn now to ask a question," Kai said.

"But you never answered mine."

"I gave you two answers."

Dane watched the way Kai's lips moved, pink and soft and full, and couldn't hold back the thought of what it would feel like to kiss them. He had a nice mouth, wide and sweet if a bit haughty. He wasn't the type to jump forward so quickly, but this was a date. And Dane's mind could not help but go there.

"I don't believe your answers."

"Well, you don't have to. So, tell me one of your earliest fantasies. A gay one, please."

Dane rolled his eyes. "I pick dare."

Those lovely lips curved upward, more sly than sweet. "Really? How disappointing."

Dane didn't like it that Kai kept responding to his comments with more questions. As if he believed Dane was the one keeping secrets. But Dane was who he was, and Kai had bid on him knowing that. Kai was the hidden one here.

Maybe that was a clue—

Before he could think further on that, Kai said, "Dare it is, then. You have to come sit on the floor at my feet. Don't worry, the rug is nice and soft."

For a few seconds, Dane did not move. He looked down at the plush contours of the black rug, felt the way it cushioned his feet, and had no objections to it. What he objected to was the position Kai demanded. *At my feet.*

"How about if I sit right here on the floor?" Dane pointed to his own feet.

"You're not allowed to negotiate on a dare," Kai said.

"Says who?"

"The rules."

And that was when Dane heard it. The tone in Kai's voice changed; it dropped low on the first comment, but higher on the second, drawing out the word *rules.*

The strong sensation returned that he had heard that voice before. Quick scenes strobed his mind. In his memory, he saw a friend of his from high school named Erik. Erik had been a jock, but not top of his game. He was near-wild and strode through the school halls as if he owned everything around him. He partied hard and was never boring.

Dane wasn't sure why Erik hung with him. Maybe because they were both part of the popular crowd, though Erik was in sports and Dane in drama. Or maybe because Dane was angry and fueled with smart and clever remarks.

It was a time in his life when his parents had divorced and he'd been finding his way through puberty without a firm father figure. Those teen years between age fourteen and seventeen that made boys—and girls, too—sometimes want to disappear into the wildness of the world and take responsibility for nothing. Erik, at sixteen, had a hot car and

Dane liked driving about in it all night long from one kid's house to the next, crashing parties or seeing who was sleeping with whom. They weren't really looking for danger so much as excitement.

Why Dane's mind flashed on Erik, he didn't know. Kai and Erik did not look a thing alike.

Wincing at the added mystery, Dane got up and sat on the floor with his back to the edge of the couch about a foot away from Kai's legs and looked straight ahead.

Nothing happened. What did he expect anyway? Kai did not move. All the seating change managed to accomplish was placing Kai at a physically higher perspective. As if Dane was now the pet.

The proximity of Kai, and where Dane was, had an added effect, though. An unexpected rush of heat came over him. Quick stings of pleasure prickled the insides of his arms, legs and stomach.

Dane stared at the tall orange flames of the fire. "My turn."

No response. No movement.

"Have you met me before?"

"Dare," came Kai's immediate reply.

Damn.

Dane thought hard. He should have planned on Kai's elusiveness.

His mind decided on a clever request. "I dare you to tell me if you've met me before."

"That's not how this works."

Dane didn't like this game. Never had. Even in high school. Or before. It might be harmless to nine year olds, but once puberty hit, the game was never about anything but making people feel uncomfortable, because the underlying current was always about sex. Always.

When dealing with other teens, sex was the focus of every joke, innuendo, gossipy rumor or even a compliment. It was about who liked who, who was fucking who, if there was more booze in someone's parent's cupboard so they could get drunk and not worry so much about the fucking going on, or what they had already done or what they were missing.

Dane never went as far as his friend Erik in these matters, but he liked to live vicariously through the guy, thinking him brave for bedding two girls in a night while Erik's real girlfriend, a good girl, was at home doing her homework.

Erik even hinted that boys were good for sucking cocks if you closed your eyes. Dane, though excited at the thought, had never known him to actually be with another boy. And Erik had never indicated he had even the slightest interest in Dane.

It was a relief, for Dane did not like Erik in that way, and at that age still wasn't sure he was gay despite his private fantasies. He liked Erik for the excitement of his lifestyle, but Erik was not the type that populated Dane's fantasies when he dreamed of boys. Erik was not the type of friend that Dane felt he could trust. Not completely. Not enough to ever let on that he might secretly like boys.

He'd been angry as a kid, and hanging with Erik gave him the push to be meaner, to laugh at his peers, to make kids squirm at the butt end of nasty jokes and run home pissed off, afraid, or even hurt. Those were his blurry teen years when he was frustrated about his parents, confused about his own internal feelings but hoping it was a phase, and terrified he wasn't cool enough to even be Erik's friend.

He wasn't angry now. He wasn't that kid anymore. He was still insecure in many ways, as anyone was, but not with triple the anxiety that being a teenager brought to it.

"Well?" Kai prompted.

Dane came out of his reverie. Wow, where had all those memories come from? One visit to his hometown for charity and he was uncontrollably reminiscing? He could not think of any clever dare to ask of Kai.

"Sit down on the floor next to me," Dane said.

"That's your dare for me?"

"Yeah. And take off your shoes."

"Oh, now we're getting somewhere. Strip Truth or Dare?"

Dane felt a half-smile crook the left side of his mouth. The couch cushions moved against his back. A scent of wine mixed with expensive cologne waved by him as Kai slid down at his side onto the plush, black rug and kicked off his black, slip-on Ferragamos. His black-stockinged feet pushed the shoes far under the long, low coffee table.

Dane picked up his wine and downed the last peppery tart drop. Then he, too, pushed off his shoes, liking the way the rug felt against the soles of his feet through his thin socks.

Kai drank the rest of his red wine and turned to look at Dane.

Dane did not meet his gaze, but stared instead at the crackling fire, and the way the big logs had split to reveal lava-orange centers. Still, out the corner of his eye he saw the fine face with its strong chin held high, skin smooth and tan, eyes wide as if questioning.

He couldn't be sure Kai was questioning with his look. He was not looking directly at him. On purpose. That was also part of the game. Part of Truth or Dare. Don't dare look too close. Don't let a guy who seems to resent you, and who looks familiar, get under your skin and make you wonder, or worry. Those were the unspoken rules. But real nonetheless. Those rules existed for self-preservation.

After a minute, Kai jumped up without a word, startling Dane. He swiftly left the room and Dane heard a low, quick conversation, a door shutting, and then he was back in about thirty seconds, a bottle of red wine in one hand, a bottle of white in the other.

Dane truly did not need more wine in his system. The night was strange enough as it was, but he said nothing as Kai filled their glasses, which flickered alternately gold and red in the firelight.

40

Kai sat on the floor again next to Dane, which felt companionable but probably was more about the game, and being fair and honorable. Dane wanted to study him, to try to solve the mystery of him, but to stare would be rude. He took a breath and held it, deliberately blanking his thoughts.

Kai said, "What made you decide to auction yourself off on a blind date?"

"It was for charity."

"No." He shook his head. "It's something more. It was a small time deal in a suburban community center. You could have written them a check. But they asked and you said yes. Do you simply say yes to everything and figure out the details later? Or do you like keeping busy? Or do you like the attention? Was it for your resume? Or were you lonely?"

Kai was brimming with energy, even when he was still. Dane's mind had quieted and even the rapid-fire questions did not bother him, but the silence in his head again allowed a brush of familiarity. Something edged his thoughts, tapping, wanting in. A memory that made his body both tense and hot at the same time.

"I thought I would be doing a good thing, that's all," Dane replied, voice low.

"Nah, it's gotta be more than that. You are around excitement and activity in your job. You don't need that, so what? Not just doing good. No one does good without some payback, or they'd do it anonymously and never tell anyone. They wouldn't take it as a tax write-off. If it was only for the well-being of others, and no extra credit, people wouldn't think twice. They'd just do the good thing and walk way and not even think of it again. But who in the world of humans is completely pure like that?"

"Do you believe that? That people cannot be inherently good? That they need some reward?" Dane asked.

"Most definitely. They need a reason. Brownie points in Heaven. Impressing an admirer. Stuffing for the ego."

Dane rubbed his palm over his bent knee, then stretched his legs out under the table. "That's a damn dark view."

"I suppose. But what proof do you have to the contrary? Give me one example. One will do."

Dane picked up his wine glass and sipped. He'd thought to stop drinking after the last glass, but now he wanted it. He wanted to lose himself. He did not know how much longer this date would last, but he was not going to be the one who chickened out, went back on the deal. The client was in charge. Short of sleeping with him, he would give the guy what he paid for.

"Monks? Nuns? The Dalai Lama?"

"The first two wear a uniform, identify with the label, present themselves to their god and commit to him. Their acts of submission give a return on their investment. They pray and live in the ecstasy of their obsession and assurance of an afterlife. The Dalai Lama would probably scoff and say he wasn't all that good, or any more good than another human being. But his gift is that he is aware of that."

Dane sighed. "I don't know, then. It's all dark and corrupt, I guess. I think most people try to do their best."

"I don't know." Kai's voice was faint.

"I don't know where you're leading with this. If you have something to say to me, just say it. You know who I am and you planned this evening. And now you think I did all of this for the attention. Why bid on me?"

"Maybe I just wanted a date with a beautiful guy."

Dane huffed. "You resented me the moment you walked into the dining room. You know me, and you won't tell me how you know me or why I'm here. But I'm here. And I must say I really like your wine." He drank another gulp.

"You know," Kai said, playing with his own glass of dark red. "Models are supposed to be stupid."

"Oh?" He wondered if he should feel insulted, but the wine—or maybe the fact that this was just a charity date—made him not care.

"Yeah. Entirely vapid. Haven't you heard that?"

"I've heard that. Doesn't make it true." Dane frowned, trying to figure out if Kai was baiting him. Then thought, *Well, of course he is. He's been toying with me all night. As if I should know something he knows but have no clue of!*

The wine was expensive and strong, and lovely how it made his head turn slower than his gaze when he moved to face Kai, knees coming up, one bumping the underside of the table. Hard.

Dane pressed his palm into the softness between them, that black rug that could double as a mattress, perhaps, and moved more onto his hip. He leaned close now, and Kai made a face, a small frown, and leaned a little away as if taken by surprise by this move.

"You like dating vapid people?" Dane asked.

"Never." Kai met his gaze, the light eyes almost cold in their gray-green appraisal.

"Then why am I here?" He shook his head. "If you think that about models, why me?"

Kai kept that smug tilt to his firm, pink lips and did not speak.

"Why? What is it you're not telling me?" Dane moved closer.

Kai put one hand up as if to ward him off, chest-level. "You—" he started to say. "It doesn't matter."

Dane watched him, the way he held himself so stiffly, how his body twisted a little at the shoulders, a held-back indecisiveness of power mixed with an almost furious frustration, all just under the surface. The green eyes moved side to side. His chest was still, as if he barely breathed. As if Kai was backed into a corner by a bigger guy. And in a way, he was.

A flash of memory came, like a fast bronze light trying to coat Dane's mind. But it was gone again, quick as it came.

"What's the story here? What is it? Please just tell me!" Dane's voice raised in volume on that last sentence. He didn't care if Kai could smell the wine on his breath. He didn't care that there was a heat forming between them, like little licking flames against thighs, hips and arms where their sides almost but did not quite touch.

Kai was very attractive. He had a harder edge, older-looking in his gaze, almost sly, but he was handsome enough he could have been a model in his own right. If he'd gone that route. If he'd wanted it badly enough—the starving, the daily gym visits, the endless attention to every detail, how the make up sought out and corrected every flaw, how the way they made him pose enhanced or decreased certain traits. And all of it airbrushed afterward anyway, as if he wasn't good enough. As if his true self, his beauty they all touted, was still never enough.

Dane looked at Kai and saw a hint of a crease at the edge of the left side of his mouth, the smooth dent in the center of the chin, the brief, pale dusting of freckles on his tanned upper cheeks--sweet kisses from the sun you'd never notice if you weren't close up--the way his hair curled taller along the right side of his forehead and fell more unruly at the left.

Again the memory-flash. And it was gone.

"Will you even tell me your full name?"

"No. And don't you dare move any closer."

The hand Kai still had up between them sported a gold ring on the middle finger with a smooth, green stone tangled with stripes of pink.

Dane had an urge to grab that hand and squeeze it, unsure if he meant to harm him or pull him closer. Kai was a very frustrating guy!

Dane bowed his head, breathing in roughly. "I'll learn your name eventually."

Kai gave him a rather rude smile.

Dane had another urge. To punch that smile right off his face. But he didn't do things like that. He wasn't that guy—

He lifted his face again, falling a little forward. Dane could take that smile another way. He could—

Kai's hand impacted with Dane's chest, not hard but like a warning tap. Dane let his upper body fall forward a little more. Until he could smell the red wine, and the cloying edge of that smoky cologne the guy wore—it made his mouth water—and Kai seemed to be raising his body up just a little, shoulders back against the couch, pushing himself. Like he suddenly didn't want to be there. Or for all his earlier bravado, he was increasingly nervous.

But Kai was just Dane's type, and something about the wine gave him courage. He could even feel a faint sort of rustling inside himself as barriers he usually kept tight and controlled started to dissolve. He put more weight on his hand at the rug, and held his other arm close to his waist as he went for it.

The brush of lip to lip, like his errant memory, came and went fast as if a shadow briefly dashed itself against his mouth.

Kai turned his head with a hiss, moving away, almost crawling on his hands and knees. His shoulder brushed Dane's shoulder, the heat between them rocketing up and leaving behind a lesser warmth but still enough that Dane could not deny it as only imagined.

"Do you think this is *that* kind of date?" Kai exclaimed.

Dane leaned on the side of his hip, watching the back of Kai's bowed head. The body language spoke of an almost-panicked state, but Kai stayed where he was, not moving, just turned away. It appeared he did not want to leave, but he did not wish to look at Dane, either.

"I'm sorry. I don't know what this is," Dane muttered, trying to keep his voice low, soft. "You brought me here."

45

The tingle remained on his lips, as if he'd just tasted something delightful that his body demanded more of. A hint of autumn breeze. A touch of suppleness. The gentle spice of skin.

He knew he could not have been completely off interpreting Kai. But the strangeness between them—some other connection was also there. Yet, he could not deny a physical attraction. And Kai had spoken of his beauty so it was mutual.

"I was hoping—" Kai began, then stopped.

"Hoping for what? Why won't you tell me?"

Kai relaxed against the back of the sofa again, and looked at him. His eyebrows were narrowed, not in a frown but more of a plea. "You don't—"

"What?"

Dane wanted to get up and leave. Not have to worry or wonder. But Kai kept him riveted, not just the allure of his features and luxurious home and the drama of bringing him here in a limo, but some inner need there behind the eyes, in the shape of his arms crossed at his sternum, the way his lips parted to show a thin shadow between them of—what?— surprise? Disappointment? Intrigue?

"You don't see people like me," Kai stated.

"What? What are you talking about?"

Dane saw him fine. Kai was the one who'd worn the hoodie in the auditorium. Who had refused to greet him face to face in the dining room. Who kept himself turned away.

"But now you see me, don't you? Because of the trappings."

"I don't understand," Dane said. He'd talked with him. He'd played Kai's child's game. He'd put up with the insults about vapid models. He'd kissed him.

Kai gave a soft, rather pretty smile. "People like you—"

Dane shook his head. More insults? "People like me? I'm just—"

Now it was his turn not to finish a sentence.

46

Kai finished for him. "Just a guy who everyone sees with the perfect face and the perfect body, right? Yeah, the attention-seeker—"

"That's not fair!" Hand flat against the rug, Dane's fingers drove into it, gripping the plush depths. "I'm not perfect. I'm not seeking anything. You don't know me. Don't keep pretending you do."

"You chose your job. Everyone looks at you and you can't deny it feels nice."

"It does, but the job is the job. I can do it so I do. It wasn't easy to get it, lots of competition. But I didn't do it just to be stared at. The pay is damn good. The benefits are phenomenal."

"Of course they are. You can probably bed whoever you want, whenever you want, party all night, wake at two in the afternoon."

"I—"

Dane watched the play of emotions across Kai's smooth face. Still wanting him even in the midst of the insults. Or maybe they were simple misunderstandings. Whichever, Dane decided he liked it that the guy had some resistance to him, and secrets. Definitely secrets.

"It's not like that just because I'm a model," Dane continued. "You don't know. Besides, anyone can party all night if they choose. And you, what about you in this ritzy house and with your own company that you invented at such a young age? You're handsome and successful, so I could say the same of you."

"Me?" Kai laughed, which was nice because it immediately relaxed the atmosphere between them. For the moment. "I'm just some nerd. Always was. Smart enough, yes. It's ironic that to finally be seen I had to do more than just create a successful company. I had to dress it up, dress the part, alter my appearance, hair, nice clothes, visits to the gym. Because invisibility remains even if you do your best, even if you are rich, unless you flaunt it. You should know."

"I should know?"

"Well, maybe you wouldn't know. Being visible your whole life. The advantages of having an appearance that generates good first impressions, or any impression at all."

"I didn't grow up like that," Dane protested.

"No?"

"And you're not a nerd. Most certainly not."

"Like that's a bad thing anyway. But you're wrong." His eyes lost a little of their flare. "I was. I still am. Inside." He patted his chest.

"We all have awkward times in our lives." As he spoke, Dane was distracted by trying to picture Kai as a nerd. He had such a lovely appearance, held himself up and proud if a little tight around the mouth, and that dark golden hair, that smooth skin, all there to attract whatever it might be that Kai wanted.

And what did Kai want? The answer came in a dizzying blast. For wasn't it obvious? Kai had spent thousands of dollars for it. For what he wanted. Tonight. But if that was true, then why were they arguing? Why was Kai resentful, resistant, and so annoyingly standoffish?

"Look," Dane said. "It's not that easy for anyone. Ever."

Dane gazed into those beautiful eyes that had lost their luster for a moment. It was a loss to the whole world that they should look like that, that Kai should ever experience a dampening of his fiery attitude, the persona in which he'd walked into that dining room like a sparkling flame, dressed to the nines, ruling the kingdom of a world he'd made while still in the bloom of incredible youth.

Again, his mind tried to supply an image of Kai any other way. A nerd? It could not be possible. But of course, as Dane has just said, everyone went through awkward stages. Some never emerged. It still did not mean they did not deserve everything they wanted in life. But as unfair as life was, deserving and achieving were two different things.

48

"Not easy for anyone," Kai echoed in a strange voice. "Easy for you to say."

"You keep talking as if you know me, as if—" Dane paused. That hesitation in the way Kai spoke, the way his voice had gone up a little, like a past fear trying to break through a newer world of mansions and fine lawns, butlers and great-rooms with ten-foot high hearths made of semi-precious stones.

Dane focused his gaze, the muscles about his eyes stiffening. He looked at Kai, who looked back with a more open gaze now, and saw a super-imposed image of stiff blond hair, stringy and unkempt, hanging across one eye, draping one cheek, and saw dark-rimmed glasses with a crack on one side. Some kid from his past. Short and skinny, gripping his books that had fallen from a torn backpack, little ripped notes from inside the backpack flying off in a gust of wind.

It had been a rainy day. Back in what grade? Ninth? Tenth? Earlier? Later? It was all a blur. But Erik was there. He remembered that much.

Why was he remembering that day, that kid?

Dane looked up at the ceiling, trying to see the image play out. Certainly Kai was not that same kid.

Was he?

He could not even remember the skinny guy's name.

"I—" Dane began. "You do know me, don't you? From high school maybe?"

"You cannot remember that which is invisible to you." Kai said the words coldly, as if recited from some psych journal. Or maybe something he'd heard on a talk show.

"No, no, I was just thinking you are familiar but, no I don't think you're right. I would have remembered someone like you."

"Someone like you."

Kai was echoing his statements again.

Dane heard a voice but it wasn't his.

Smart-ass, showing me up in class like that!

He saw the stringy-haired boy's face in his mind again, pinched, terrified, jerking to move as if to run after his papers, but too frozen or too shocked to move, losing the moment. Losing everything to that ugly moment behind broken glasses and messy hair, trying so hard to lift his chin, to square his shoulders—

Just like Kai had done when Dane had leaned to kiss him, and afterward, moving away, almost crawling, then stopping to face him but with an open look no longer filled with resentment, but dismay.

Yes, it was dismay now that parted those perfect pink lips, that frosted the green-gray in the eyes to a tinted silver gleam.

"I remember a boy," Dane heard himself saying. He interrupted his own thought with a demand for logic. It was infuriating that the memory would not come in full color with more details and dialog and names. "Did we go to school together?"

Kai sat with his head bowed now, face in shadow. He folded his hands in his lap, rotating his thumbs under and over each other. Staring at them.

"It's stupid of me, I know, to expect you to remember."

"So just tell me!"

"Hush and I will." The voice came soft, head still bowed, thumbs nervously circling each other.

Dane gulped. The fire whispered and crackled. The shadows in the room took on a thicker hue, tan to brown to gray, as if bending close to listen. Dane's body tensed. His back felt hot.

"I remember every detail about you. I don't know why I'd expect you to remember the same." Kai's voice came in an almost-whisper.

Dane sighed.

Kai held up one hand. "Shut up. Don't speak. I told myself for the longest time you were just an idiot kid. We all were. But I didn't want to believe it. Because I remember it all, and you. I remember you. And I know you don't. I know you don't remember. And it's not your fault that when I saw your billboards, your pictures, you, I resented it. You. There. Out in the world. Being seen. Visible. It's not your fault that I hoped you weren't so shallow, still such an idiot."

"What the fuck?" Dane asked. "What are you talking about?"

It seemed Kai could not speak plainly about this, though. It was too close to him, somehow, or too important. And memories were also like that, snapshot slices of life, not full-bodied, containing what the mind decides to decipher them as, define them to be, representing moments in life that signal fear, hate, trauma, love, awakening.

Everything the mind saw was affected by these prejudices, the emotions of the moment, the perceptions that defined the reality. A reality that was as different and unique for each person as a thumbprint, as a personality emerging since the moment of reason at age three, four, or five.

"I don't mean to insult you," Kai said. "But you did hang with a rather insipid crowd, exciting maybe, but unable to formulate much more than rudimentary thought processes like whose house can I party at next, where's my next beer coming from, what girl will let me fuck her in what car's back seat. But I remember you, Dane. I hoped you might have other thoughts. I dreamed—" He stopped for a breath. Swallowed. "I don't think you can even halfway conceive of the reason why I do remember, or begin to understand what I did."

"You knew me?" Dane saw the stringy-haired, skinny kid again. But that kid was silent in his mind. Had they ever said two words to each other? He didn't think so. He would have remembered. He wasn't that horrible of a kid even when he was angry and rude and wild in those years after his parents split up and he had thought the world might just rear up and swallow him whole.

"Yes. But you obviously did not know me," Kai replied.

"I—I don't know. Did I?"

"I said shut up. I'm trying to explain. Just shut up for a second. And then you can leave. You can go home and forget, just forget, because that is what I'll be asking you to do. That is what we both need to do, after this, is just forget about it. Forget about it at all, because really it's nobody's fault, nobody's, not yours, not mine, it was just the way of high school and teenagers and hanging out with different crowds. Your crowd was Erik and parties and starring in school plays. Mine was the chess club. Get it?"

"Not really."

Dane badly wanted Kai to look up now. He wanted to see his face again, make sure it wasn't looking as broken as the turn of the voice. He had not expected this from this evening. But now here he was, and he would listen, and he would learn and try to remember. Because this guy had, for some reason, paid four thousand dollars for this very moment. This confrontation. And Dane would make sure he got his money's worth.

"So," Kai continued. "I remember every detail and you don't. Sue me. We all remember different things. Things that have impact. Certainly, I am under no false illusions that I made any impact at all. But I can't help it that you made an impact. That you were a world I could not have no matter what, that I might have wanted once, and expecting that you would feel the same, it's so dumb. But I do remember. I have that flaw. And I can't unmake that flaw, or fix it. So when I saw you again, after all these years, modeling underwear, and heard about the auction, well, I came. I bid. I won."

Dane heard a small smile in that voice, yet it probably bittered those pink lips with a faint, quivery grimace.

"Okay," Dane said, vowing he would not be defensive, that he would listen. For this man was certainly something, and he could feel the rush of heat in his veins at the thought that he'd been on this guy's radar for more than a whimsical idea for a charity date. "Please. Just humor me. Start at the beginning. What do you remember? Why am I here? If I did something to you, I am sorry. So sorry."

"Oh, you didn't have to do anything to cause this. And you didn't. So rest easy."

Dane was not so sure he would "rest easy" but he held still and kept his silence.

"There was a day," Kai began, "in ninth grade when I first saw you." He spoke slowly.

Dane waited.

"God that Erik. He was so stupid. I wonder whatever happened to him. Anyway, we had science class together. All of us."

Dane did not recall this at all, but he accepted it anyway.

"The teacher asked the class a question about gravity and Erik said something really stupid. That it was something we could not see and therefore not a real thing, something really dumb like that. I don't remember his exact words because Erik is not worthy of remembering at all. But I started to laugh out loud. Without raising my hand, I answered the question over him, cutting him off. And after class he was real mad. Real, real mad."

Dane closed his eyes and let the words pour over him like a tepid shower, the type where the water pressure sucks and the hot water is running low and you can't decide if you are enjoying it anymore.

Kai continued. "Erik had his flunkies who followed him everywhere. Mike was one of them I remember a little. The rest are featureless. Except for you. Dane. The magnificent Dane who all the girls whispered about in the halls, and made lists about in their notebooks. Anyway, after class that day, Erik veered straight toward me, cutting me off at the boy's room."

Dane started to remember now. They'd come out of the hall where the lockers were and into a grassy area where there was a drinking fountain and, further down, some restrooms.

He remembered the kid with the backpack, alone and small and not really worth anyone's time. But how could he have thought that? Those memories had been buried but now they came and was he really that guy? The one who could actually think another person was not worth anyone's time?

But he remembered thinking it, and now his cheeks flushed.

Kai said, "I figured Erik would be pissed. And I was scared, although I didn't think he'd really hurt me. But then I saw you, like a persistent shadow behind him, sort of grinning, even, and that was all I saw. I couldn't take my eyes off you, but you weren't looking at me, and while I was distracted Erik grabbed my pack and ripped it open and everything went flying and the wind came up and it blew through all my notes and my laptop fell out and later I saw the screen had cracked, but that's not what I'm remembering. No. It was the way the wind came up and how your hair went back like a soft part of that wind, dark and shining, and your eyes so bright and blue that I couldn't look away. Except you were looking down a ways, not even at Erik, like you couldn't be bothered, like what Erik was doing affected you not in the least. But I was affected. Not by Erik. But by you."

Now Kai pushed himself up so that he was squatting and took his seat again on the couch, as if being on the floor at the same level as Dane—as the oblivious and uncaring soul that was Dane—was too disgusting.

Dane did not move. Nor did he look up. He let Kai rise above him because he knew it was deserved, and it was the only way Kai might continue now. Because the story was started and Dane had to hear the rest. He simply had to.

"After that, well, I guess Erik said foul things. I don't remember those details. I just could not get you out of my mind. You don't know the half of it. But I followed you everywhere after that. For about three years. And you never noticed. I asked people about you. I went to your plays. I learned everything I could. But I could not get up the courage to even say "hi" to you, and if you did notice, even just a little, you had not a single concern about it."

Dane pushed his hand through his hair and drew both knees up to his chest. Eyes still closed, he tried to think, to picture this little stringy-haired guy. But he couldn't, not beyond that initial memory of the spilled papers and books. Not past the moment when Erik stalked away, laughing, and Dane was caught up in his energetic wake as if nothing could be bad about Erik because of that charisma, that way he had of controlling every situation and everyone around him.

"You followed me around?"

"When I could."

"But you should have, you should have—"

"Should have what?" Kai interrupted.

"Introduced yourself, said 'hi'. I wasn't a bad kid. I wasn't."

Silence.

Now Dane opened his eyes. The fire blithely danced, as if the world held nothing but fire itself to admire. His wine glass winked amber, gold, green. He was aware of Kai's legs over the edge of the couch, close enough to touch if he reached out.

As if sensing his thought, Kai pulled his legs up and crossed them, out of Dane's line of peripheral vision.

Dane turned, looking up. Kai was staring straight ahead.

Dane said, "I would have said 'hi' back."

It seemed as if Kai did not hear him, for Kai said, "Well, that's it then. Now you know. And now this date is over. So you can leave."

Chapter Five

Dane did not want to leave. Not now. Not after all this. Wasn't there so much more to say?

"Kai. Is that your name? Was that what you went by in high school?" He was thoroughly ashamed he could not remember.

"Kyle."

"Kyle." He cleared his throat and said the name again. "Kyle. What if I don't want to leave?"

"What if you don't have a choice?"

"Do I have a choice?" Dane asked.

Kai did not reply right away.

Dane pushed himself up on the side of the couch, sliding his ass up and onto the soft, leather cushions, leaning back. Now they were on the same level again. It was necessary for this to be on one level now. For all of it.

Kai spoke. "No. You don't have a choice. I don't want you here. Not anymore."

For a second Dane thought he had mis-heard Kai. He couldn't not want him here. He'd spent so much money for this moment. To finally meet. To have his say.

"I don't understand."

"Of course you wouldn't understand. After everything I told you—"

"But that's the past. We're grown up now. Adults."

"Yes. With free will and everything. And now I am saying I don't want you here."

It might have felt like a slap in the face, but Dane was too stunned. Kai had gone to all this trouble just to throw him out? It was more Erik's fault than anyone's. Kai had the right to be angry. Even to this day. But Erik had been the one to rip the backpack, shove him, call him names. Not Dane.

"Erik really was a dick. I have to agree with you."

Kai let out a muffled laugh, but did not sound at all amused. "I was not talking about Erik. In fact, I have nothing to say about Erik. He's a game piece in my memory and nothing more. Not flesh and blood. In fact, I'm pretty sure he doesn't have a heart. I have no thought toward him at all. It's you, Dane. You I was talking about. And it figures you couldn't even hear that from me. Not at all."

"That's not fair. I heard you. But I didn't know, I didn't see—"

"That's just it. You let that guy rule you, control you, even. To the point where you didn't see, probably on purpose, the things he did. And that makes you, well, sort of a dick, too, don't you think? And so now I'm asking you to leave."

Quite suddenly, Dane's body heated again, but this time with utter embarrassment. Everything surrounding him responded to that crawling discomfort. The couch was no longer soft and yielding, but slippery and cold. The fire mocked him with flame fingers pointed and shaking at him in judgment. Even the food from the fine dinner roiled in his belly as if to say, "I reject you."

He wasn't wanted. He wasn't wanted here and never had been.

He lifted himself up, his head wavering for a moment. Too much wine. Too much memory.

"I'm sorry," he said, voice scratching, making him even more chagrined. "I'll leave."

He shouldn't care. This was a singular sort of vendetta from someone he really did not know. Why should he care?

But something had been awakened in him by the evening, by the silly game of Truth or Dare, by the meal, the wine, the fire. And the kiss. He had felt something. A compatibility at least. Maybe more. A chemistry rare to find, perhaps.

He'd been fascinated by Kai since Kai had walked in the door. And now it was his loss to bear that Kai did not want anything to do with him because of some ignorant act at age fifteen. At an age when life and puberty and everything teens find painful had distracted him.

He apologized again. "I'm sorry."

Kai did not look up. "Get out."

"I like you, Kai. It was a good dinner and I thank you for it." Dane tried to think of more to say, something kind. But everything he thought of in the moment seemed lame. "I wish I'd had the chance to get to know you. Honestly, I don't know what else to say."

"I don't want you to say anything. I want you to get out."

Dane nodded, though Kai would not see it with his head turned away.

It was all too funny. Too strange. Kissing Kai had felt different from any other kiss he'd ever had. More than experimentation or lust or drunken fun. He hadn't had many guys in his bed, but there was a reason. None of them quite appealed. They didn't make his heart pick up or his skin tremble. They didn't interest him beyond a level of curious and quick fumblings in the dark to scratch a biological itch. But Kai was different. With an energy that made him feel a keener focus, an urge to know more.

They barely knew each other, but still a hollowness welled up at this missed opportunity.

Dane wondered if the limo was still waiting. Certainly he needed a ride back to the community theatre, to his left-behind car. A twenty minute drive through the darkened nighttime, alone. It was autumn dark, and he was going home alone.

Stupid. Why would he ever have thought he wouldn't be going home alone anyway?

He slipped on his shoes and rose, moving swift and silent to the closed door of the living room, opening it onto the small, bare hall.

58

There was no sound throughout the whole house. Not even from the nice butler Ben.

Well, he knew his own way out. He would go down the hall and through the room that showed off the grand twin staircases. Beyond that, the foyer led to the stained glass doors, and the dragonflies that colored the surface. Then the night would enfold him. And he could go into it and forget again. Just forget.

That was the moment he realized he'd left his jacket. He didn't need his jacket. It was an expensive suit, but he didn't care. He'd get another.

He started to turn. Froze.

Footsteps came from the other side of the house. Blinking, he moved quicker now, past the stairs, the walls of art, and the front table with the orchids. The dragonflies seemed to shiver, their wings trembling.

He opened the front door, and the vast yard and trees were all shadows now, dim and black and dark gray. The air smelled of woodsmoke. And spice. The fire he'd just left behind. And the man.

He closed the door softly behind him, seeing the limo waiting by the raining fountain. The driver was playing with his phone, the light of it making his face almost ghoulish, white and blue and faint green.

Dane skipped rapidly down the brick steps and knocked on the bright, front window of the long, sleek vehicle.

The driver's head jerked upward, turning toward him. He reached for a side door button and the window rolled open.

"Sir?"

"I need to get back to my car," Dane said.

"Of course, sir." The chauffeur started to open his door.

"I'll just ride up front if you don't mind," Dane said.

"Yes, sir."

Dane reached for the handle and opened the door. Before he got in, a breeze came up and ruffled his hair, loosening his bangs. It was cool and fresh and for a moment he flashed back on the kid with the stringy hair, the papers flying about in a sudden wind gust. He had seen that happen. He had noticed. He did remember. He just hadn't known the kid's name. And he hadn't thought of him, or that incident, in years.

With the houselights at his back, and the pretty pole lamps glimmering white through their rectangular glass panes, his path was clear. He was leaving. He was going home. Alone.

Kai hated him. For a thoughtless, childhood incident, Kai hated him.

Kyle. That was the kid's name, although not his full name. He remembered Erik's words better now. All of them. How they rode the wind with arrogance and amusement. And anger. *Smart-ass, showing me up in class like that! Kyle the creep, isn't that what they call you? Kyle the know-it-all. Kyle the suck-up.*

Dane remembered how he pretended those words, which were very cruel, didn't matter. They were just words. The kid was fine. The kid would not care. He was getting straight A's. He'd be somebody one day. And Erik, well, everyone knew Erik was a blowhard. Funny, even. Crass and blunt. But no one ever took Erik's words to heart, did they?

But for that, Dane was being kicked out on his ass after a charity auction that cost his date a lot of money. For that, Dane was called to be present and suddenly hated. No, not suddenly. But he hadn't known he was hated until now.

He stooped and got into the front passenger seat of the limo.

The chauffeur had already turned on the engine and the limo purred as it started to roll around the drive, smooth as driving on silk even on the cracked and uneven flagstones of pink and dirty quartz.

"Did you have a good dinner?" the chauffeur asked. He glanced with a friendly smile toward Dane, both hands turning the wheel.

"Fine."

"Sir, did you not have a jacket when you arrived?"

"It doesn't matter."

"I see."

The man seemed to sense that Dane was unhappy and, yes, he was and it wasn't fair. The entire evening wasn't fair. He'd been bought. He'd been discarded. He wished he'd never volunteered for the auction in the first place and simply written them a check.

But then he remembered something else. Something Kai had said just before he'd ended the date.

I followed you everywhere. For about three years. And you never noticed.

Kai had liked him.

I asked people about you. I learned everything I could.

Kai had more than "liked" him. Kai had had a crush on him after the incident. Kai had not hated him.

The lamplight along the drive slid over the windshield in dark watercolors of blues and golds. Dane put his hands on his knees and nervously rubbed his palms. It was cool out but he felt quite hot.

The dash on the limo let out a few loud dings.

"Seatbelt, please," said the driver, shrugging as if he was apologizing.

Dane started to reach for it over his right shoulder and stopped.

"Wait." Dane pulled his hand back.

The driver looked over at him, the car slowing.

"Stop," said Dane.

"Going back for your jacket after all?" asked the driver.

"No. I mean, yes. I mean—just stop."

The car came to rest just where the flagstones ended and the black pavement that made up the rest of the driveway began. Dane pulled the handle on the door and it opened. The interior light came on, bathing them in pale light. Cool air wafted in.

Dane got out without another word and turned around once, looking up at the dark sky and the stars. They were bright from his vantage on this hill, but still dimmed by the surrounding city lights from all the suburbs that stretched without a break fifty miles west into Los Angeles. He took a deep breath of the air, fresh and flowery but dusty as always in southern California, and straightened his tense body. He took a step forward, facing the house.

The windows watched him, some dark and secretive, some coppery with edges of pink that hinted at life within.

Dane strode toward the front porch and the dragonfly doors that looked shut and dark now, uninviting. His shoes kicked at the hard flagstones as he walked, a quiet tapping. When he reached the silent bushes alongside the steps, the flowery fragrance grew stronger. White blooms glowed intermittently throughout the shadowed plants.

Now the doors stood closed a foot from him, and he reached up to ring the bell. One ring. That was all.

He waited for what seemed like long minutes. He heard the limo make the circle and drive up to the front again, idling softly.

Finally, he heard footsteps echo from within the house. The door opened. Ben stood looking at him, illuminated from behind by white interior light, the softer grays in his hair turning silver. He had something in his hand and held it out.

For a moment, Dane could not make out what it was. He blinked.

"Your jacket, sir," said Ben.

"What?"

"You left your jacket behind."

Dane frowned. "I didn't come back for my jacket."

Ben held it out, unmoving, as if unsure what to do.

"I came back to see Kai. I—I forgot to tell him something. I need to tell him something."

"I'm sorry, sir. I have strict instructions from the owner not to let you into this house. Ever. I apologize."

Stunned, Dane could not move. For a moment everything dissolved around him, the house, the butler, the steps beneath his feet, the dusky scents of west coast autumn. He saw only rolling shadows out his peripheral vision, and a blinding whiteness before him.

"Sir?"

Dane heard the butler's voice as if from far away.

"Sir? Please take your jacket. The chauffeur will drive you home."

Dane shook his head to clear it. "No, I—"

"Sir, please. I need to close this door now."

"Ben," Dane began, as the world slowly re-formed. "If you could just tell him I need to see him. Just for a minute. Please."

Ben gave a long sigh. "Please take your jacket, sir. I'm sorry."

Dane did not move.

Sighing again, Ben pushed it onto his arms, draping it a little over his shoulder. Then he stepped back and shut the door with a gentle click right in Dane's face.

For a moment Dane stood watching the shadow of the receding butler through the colored shapes of glass, listening to the limo purring less than twenty feet off waiting to whisk him away as if this day had never happened. As if this world on the hill in the middle of the suburbs was only a dream.

Why had he gone back anyway? His current lifestyle and job provided him with choices that included meeting a lot of wealthy people in houses on hills in places even more ritzy than this. But that wasn't what this "dream" was about that he was waking from. That wasn't why he'd jumped out of the limo and come back.

He had not finished this yet. This meeting with Kai. This charity date. This strangely alluring autumn evening with a man—and now a past memory of a boy—he could not get out of his mind.

He wanted to tell Kai he was sorry again. He wanted to explain his side of the story, that his teen life had been about wildness and distraction and looking away from people, not toward them. That his parents' divorce had shattered him more than he could define at that age. That he had needed a bully like Erik on his side to feel important again, even if it was shallow, even if it was wrong.

He turned and looked at the sleek black limo and the polite chauffeur inside, face turned to stare at him, patiently waiting. Dane shook his head. Waved the guy on. Then he sat down on the cold stone steps, placed his jacket on his lap, his elbows on his knees, and put his head in his hands.

The hard stone against his ass was cold, but he didn't care. Maybe he'd had too much wine or something. This was quite unusual behavior for him. He did not go where he wasn't wanted. He certainly did not try to prolong dates that had gone bad.

Kai had made it perfectly clear he was throwing Dane out. So why had Dane jumped out of the limo and returned?

He wanted to explain himself. Yes. That was part of it. But something deeper was going on. A surge, a pull, a crazy longing to not only tell his side, his story, but to make up for his shortcomings somehow. His heart hurt. He frowned, letting himself feel it, and realized it was not for himself he was aching, but for Kai, for Kai's plight. He was hurting because something in Kai had hurt all those years ago, and maybe it was still hurting right now.

The man hated him. But the kid. That fourteen year old skinny boy with the backpack and brains behind unkempt blond hair had maybe, kind of, sort of loved him. Or at the very least had a crush.

And to know that, to hear Kai speak of it this evening, had sparked a thrill in Dane, and a guilty anger at himself. He couldn't change the past, but he could make his own path starting right now. He'd already been attracted to Kai from the very start. But now that he knew the full story, there was a strange, crazy delight to it that would not retreat. He wanted to see Kai again. And he didn't want to wait until it was too late and the night was over and they'd both forgotten how for a moment they'd been intrigued with each other. There had been a connection. Hadn't there?

The limo did not pull away, much to Dane's annoyance. Instead, the driver got out, leaving his door open, and walked over to Dane.

"Sir?"

"I know. I'm not wanted. I'm probably crazy. But I'm not ready to leave yet. So I'm just going to sit here for awhile. You can leave. I have a cell. I'll call a cab when I'm ready to go."

"I am instructed to take you back to your car. I can't just leave you here in the dark."

"Go on. I can take care of myself," Dane said.

"It's not that, sir, but that my client has specific and strict instructions."

Dane looked up at the driver. "Look. I'll find my own way home. And no matter what your client has told you to do, you can't force me into that limo."

"Okay, okay." He put his hands up, backing away a step. The gravel crunched under his polished, black shoes.

Dane bowed his head into his hands again. He heard the chauffeur walk away, the scratching footsteps, the slam of the driver's door, the hum of the limo and the crackling of the tires on the flagstones as it slowly pulled away.

Long after the limo was gone, Dane sat, palms pressed to his cheeks, and he simply let the sounds of the evening encompass him, the crickets, the fluttering of leaves in a small breeze, and the distant rumble of all the surrounding cities that sprawled from Los Angeles all the way to the desert in the east. Behind him, the house was quiet. He did not hear even the thump of a settling window or board.

But Kai was in there. And so was Ben. And there had been two servants at dinner. He hadn't seen them again after the dessert, so maybe they had left for the day, but even if they hadn't left, the house felt empty. Almost sad.

Faraway, an owl called, low and breathy on the air. The loneliest sound.

He stretched his legs out, chastising himself for that thought. He had no reason to think it. He wasn't lonely. His life was going great. He had a great career—even if it wasn't quite steady—and when he was working and in demand, he lived a rather fast-paced, jet-set sort of lifestyle.

Where love was concerned, he wasn't even ready for it. He didn't care for fast hook-ups, but they wouldn't have made up for his lack of love anyway. They had nothing to do with love. But he didn't care. He was young. He had plenty of time to think later about finding someone special, settling down.

So why was he hanging out on the porch steps of a guy who'd bought him—yes, bought him!—when quite obviously the guy didn't want him and the date was well and thoroughly done?

Because his heart ached in a way he had not felt since his parents' divorce. Because in this moment pride had left him and all he could see was Kai as a kid standing in the wind and hurting. And now as a man, Kai was turning away. Maybe angry. Maybe still hurt. And Dane was the reason why.

He rubbed hard at his eyes until he saw dark red dotted with white spots behind his eyelids. He ran his fingers through his hair, pressing hard against his scalp.

The air shuddered cold against his shoulders but it didn't pain him. In fact, he liked it. He wanted to feel that coldness all the way through as it seeped into him like the stone he sat on. It felt like distance. It felt like it was pulling him into a realm of echoes and longing, and something inside him opened up as if slain by a weapon forged of the very grit at the core of need.

He rocked his head up, eyes opening.

Kai stood before him.

Dane jerked back on the step. How had he not heard him? How long had Kai been standing there? The door behind him was open, leaking a drastic light across the bricks, invading the night, hurting Dane's eyes. Kai was on the bottom step, and obviously he'd walked there, but somehow, Dane had been so out of it he hadn't even heard his footsteps.

"What are you doing?" Kai demanded.

"Sitting."

"You were rude to my chauffeur."

He hadn't been rude, in truth. But he didn't want to argue.

Kai had not changed his clothes. He still wore the white shirt, though it was un-tucked from his dark trousers now. He still had a look of power, a kind of heady charisma, and even with his head tilted down and staring at Dane, there was a proud stance to him, and an ethereal beauty.

Dane's entire body nearly swooned, and heat brimmed up through the coldness in his bones to sting his veins. Kai was lovely.

"You have to leave," Kai said.

"I'm just going to sit here for awhile if that's okay with you."

"It's *not* okay. You can't just sit there on my step."

"Why not?"

"Because I asked you to leave."

"I feel like I want to explain myself to you. That I owe you even more than that. But it's a start."

Kai kicked at the step. Hard. "I don't want your explanations. You're trespassing on my property. If you don't leave, I'll call the police."

Dane frowned. "Really? The police? I'm sitting on your step trying to gather myself together. I'm not hurting anyone or anything."

"You've done enough for tonight. You don't owe me anything more, and I don't want anything more. Why won't you just leave!" Kai's hands were fists at his side. He turned away, head tilted back, as if trying to control his temper.

Dane said, "I know I'm the villain in your story, but I'm really not a bad guy."

Kai turned to look at him again. "So? What? You want me to reassure you that you're just fine, just an upstanding dude and all that? You don't need me. And fuck you anyway for expecting me to give you that sort of—of statement. Why should I?"

Kai was right, of course. Dane blinked at him, confused by his own response to this man who seemed to hate him, but who managed in one short evening to capture Dane's interest and hold it. To captivate him with his energy and quickness, his beauty and his pride. He couldn't help himself. He wanted more and he felt helpless and stupid because of it. Because Kai—angry and resentful Kai—wanted nothing more to do with him.

"I don't expect it," Dane said. "I just didn't want to leave like this, with things unfinished between us. It doesn't feel right."

"I don't give a damn what you want or what feels right to you. Why isn't that good enough for you?"

"I want to apologize again even if you don't want to hear it. For the past, I guess, but also for all of it. Anything I made you feel badly about, if I didn't notice you back then, and if now I did anything to piss you off. I want to say I'm sorry. But it's not good enough, I know. But there has to be more I can do. Can't there be more?"

Kai looked at him with half-squinted eyes, a dark glimmer in their depths.

"What more? You merely want to feel good about yourself. That's not my problem. That's your problem."

Dane put his hand up. His other hand clutched at his jacket, which dragged against the step. "Stop closing me out for just one second. Please! Just a second. A moment. That's all I ask."

"What? You want to kiss me again like you did in the living room? That's not gonna happen."

"I would never do anything you didn't want. Never." To make Kai angry again had not been Dane's intention. He glanced away, lips pressed tight, and let out a defeated sigh.

Kai turned toward the back of the drive, fists still tight against his thighs. The breeze kicked up again, scattering twigs and broken leaves, bringing with it scents of grass and a dusty edge of the turning season. Above, the stars twinkled so far away that all dreams seemed unreachable at the moment, bereft.

"Please listen to me," Dane said, pitching his voice soft. "I was a stupid kid. My parents had just divorced. I don't remember a lot. I was in a blur, half-crazed, self-destructive as many teenagers are—"

"I don't want to hear it," Kai said, interrupting. "I just don't." He sighed. "Don't talk anymore."

"What—"

"I said I don't want to hear it." Kai pursed his lips and let out his breath in a huff.

"I'm sorry." Dane's voice came in a whisper. "Of course you don't."

"There. Was that so hard to just shut up?"

Dane swallowed and blinked. Out the corner of his eye he saw Kai lift an eyebrow. The man's posture changed. He looked softer, glowing, young and alone. Dane felt it again, a slow warmth as if sparks had swept up between them. Part of it was the past, and the words exchanged that had built a tenuous, if resentful, connection. Part of it was the present moment in the dim lamplight where the night gave them both softer edges, and groomed away the more ugly vulnerabilities and left what was plain and honest. Mutual attraction. Dane felt his insides heat with the pleasant trickle of arousal. Kai took a deep breath and did not let it out and Dane knew Kai felt the same.

Dane turned his head and gazed at him, the light hair darkened to brown in the evening's shadows. The smooth, flat cheeks, the slightly opened lips.

All tension began to subside.

Kai turned until he was looking at him. He let out his breath, a soft hiss. His eyes seemed bigger with the muscles of his face relaxed.

"Walk with me. There's a path. The grounds are somewhat lit but just don't trip or anything," Kai said quietly.

Dane took a hesitant step forward, his heart leaping in his chest. But Kai did not even seem to notice Dane's relief as he spun and began walking rapidly over the flagstones toward a line of shadowed foliage and a curving darkness that wound through the lawn toward the side of the huge house. It seemed he expected Dane would follow. Dane did.

Kai's white shirt glowed in the dark. He walked fast. Dane had to lengthen his stride to keep up.

They were going for a walk. That was great. It meant their evening was not over. It meant there was still more between them that needed to play out. That could only be a good thing, Dane told himself.

Well, at the very least, he could hope it was a good thing, for now. He needed more to come from this night. Because in his heart something was expanding, aching, needing. And the catalyst for that was, undeniably, the fiery and still somewhat unfriendly presence of Kai.

Chapter Six

Tree shadows wove the air with tall bodies and long arms. The moon had begun to rise, a slice of battered stone.

Kai was moving fast, which was not conducive to walking and talking. Dane had hoped for more talking. He wasn't done explaining himself, damn it.

Dane thought about what Kai said, accusing Dane of wanting to make excuses so he could feel better about himself. But that was like saying he was devoid of empathy, that he didn't care about Kai feelings, too. He wanted to tell Kai that he did care, that he was sorry, not to manipulate Kai into forgiving him, but so Kai might understand that Dane did not approve of causing pain to anyone.

But any way he looked at how to communicate his thoughts, they still came off defensive.

Kai's white shirt stood out like a beacon in the dark; Dane probably looked the same. They were dressed nearly alike, although Dane still had his tie, which was now loose about his neck. The cool night combed his hair, prickling his scalp.

Suddenly, in front him were stone steps set into the grass. Kai bounded up them. The outside pole lights were behind them now. Dane followed in the dim light.

Stepping stones met them as the area flattened out. An oak with low branches bowed toward the hazy pathway.

"Kai—"

Kai held up his arm without turning. A hiss of air met Dane's ears. "Hush."

They came to another copse of oaks, all dark green and gray in the night and blocking most of the sky. They did not go beneath them, for which Dane was grateful. He was afraid of spiders in their webs.

Coming into view were a series of wood benches, and a cement fire pit well away from the trees. The fire pit looked clean and un-used, except for a few husks and leaves trembling within. This place was beautiful and no doubt could be used for parties, though it was far from the gazebo on the other side of the drive. Still, campfires, a lovely yard and stately, old oaks. What could be better?

"This place," Kai began. "Sometimes I like to just come here and sit."

"Alone?"

Kai finally looked at him. "Why not? It's quiet. No one to bother me if I remember to turn off my phone. Running a big company even with good help—I've never done that before. I need breaks away from the hub-bub, the city, the people, all of it. I'm not a golfer. I don't like camping. So I come here."

Dane made a mental note to remember this. No golf. No trips to desert or mountains without a motel booked in advance.

As if there was anything between them. As if he even had a chance for that, or a future that including booking trips with Kai. But—Kai had brought him here to his special place. It was more than just about walking off some steam.

Minutes ago, Dane had sat on the stoop, his head in his hands. Tossed away with the wind. But now here they stood, apart from things, from the past, in the very now of an autumn night with nothing else to distract them. Nothing else between them but voice, and this moment. With the city behind them and the stars above.

Dane could have just walked away but it had not been possible. To leave Kai like this, with things between them undone, unsaid. He felt drawn to the man. Even now.

In the muted light, Kai's hair shone. His body looked wiry, whipchord beneath his clothing. Like it might burn Dane to touch it. Blister and peel away the outside self he showed the world to reveal his core.

72

He'd never had this response to anyone before, not even a good friend he might tell secrets to. Because he always had his pretty face, and his smile; he could charm anyone, and he leaned on that. Always.

Kai might have had a crush on him once, but he didn't seem to care much about that now. It was amazingly intriguing. This was someone who'd spent money on him possibly to prove a point. It shamed and appalled him. It enflamed him.

Kai sat abruptly on one of the benches.

Dane remained standing, kicking at a tuft of grass. He still held his jacket folded under one arm, his hand pressed against his sternum. His other hand was in his pocket, fingers curled tight. He hunched his shoulders against the cold.

Kai said, softly, "I never really forgot you. Or forgave you."

It had been ten years ago. Dane wanted to say it wasn't his fault he didn't remember much, but kept silent. Kai deserved to be heard now.

"It's easy to find out things about other kids through the grapevine. I did that. I knew you didn't keep girlfriends for more than one school dance. I knew where you lived. I knew you got A's in drama class and not such good grades in everything else. You weren't on the football team, so why'd you hang out with Erik? Why did he like you? Why did you like him? I was angry about that. And jealous. I let it consume me sometimes. But no one ever knew. And I don't know why, now, I am telling you all this, but when I saw you on the billboards I started to remember again. And I had this turmoil start up inside me again. I hated you. And I didn't hate you." He shook his head.

Dane kicked harder at the grass. He remained silent.

Kai continued. "Then I saw a poster in a nearby restaurant for the charity auction. On the list of names of minor local celebrities your name jumped right out. I thought about going and then I thought what an idiot I was. It wasn't until the last minute today that I planned all this. The dinner was easy. Ben's a good employee. The chauffeur, Mark, is someone I keep on retainer for the company. So I just thought why not buy a date with you. See what you've become. See if I still hate the thought of you. I don't know why. It was stupid. All of it. And now you know that. And why, fuck why didn't you just leave when I asked you to tonight?"

All the words came in a rush.

Dane played them over and over in his mind. Especially one part. *I hated you. I didn't hate you.* For Kai this must have been a turmoil. And for Dane, well, he didn't want to be the guy who was hated. Somehow, this was his fault. In school, he had not been an outright bully, but he had been the one who looked the other way.

"I'm not the kind of guy who leaves things open-ended on a bad note. That's why I didn't leave," said Dane. "I might be like anyone who gets caught up in the moment and does something wrong, but if I realize it I apologize. I was a stupid, crazy teenager. I have no excuses for that. But I'm not that teenager anymore. I'm an adult. I wronged you."

"I know you did. You already apologized. But you didn't like my answer to your apology. Is that why you stayed? So you can get me to say, 'it's okay', and things can go back to normal for you?"

"No." Dane said. "It's because I think you didn't hear me. The real me. Taking responsibility. I don't know what else to say." But he had more to say. What he didn't have was the words. How could he say those words and not feel insanely ridiculous. *I'm drawn to you. I think your fire burns me from within. I think, having met you, I'm becoming ash.*

"Am I supposed to thank you for that?"

So funny, but Dane was even more drawn to him for asking that question. The rejection in his voice. The underlying message that perhaps he found Dane to be insipid, or in his earlier words, a "vapid model" made Dane fueled to prove otherwise.

74

"You don't have to thank me. For anything. Ever. But I should probably thank you," Dane said.

"What, for the stupid dinner and the stupid wine and the stupid fire?" Kai sounded so forlorn.

"No. I mean, yes. For all of that. But, no, I should thank you for bringing to my attention that I can be a cold son of a bitch sometimes. Especially back then. And that maybe even now I still have that lesson to look at. To make myself better. A better person."

"And still," Kai said, snidely. "You turn this all around to make it all about you. Always. And again."

"What?" he asked, shocked by Kai's vehemence. "No. I mean, yes, it is in a way about me, about both of us. How can it not be? I needed to learn how you felt. I think you needed to meet me to teach me that. I guess. I don't know. I don't know anything, Kai. You tell me." It was frustrating. Everything got turned around on him and he wasn't a bad guy. Did he deserve this? Maybe. Maybe not. But if he was mucking this all up even worse, at least he'd tried.

"I don't know anything, either," Kai said angrily. His fist pounded the wood bench. "I don't. But what I do know right now is that I don't trust you. And those feelings are coming up again from the past and I should never have done this. I don't know what I was thinking."

Dane didn't know what he'd been thinking, either. A charity date auction. It sounded simple. But he should have known it would be at best uncomfortable, and again he thought he should have just declined politely and written a check. Well, if wishes were horses….

Taking a long breath of the fresh air, Dane walked about the fire pit and onto the grass, glancing around. He could see the side of the house where the huge patio jutted over the glistening pool. The houselights illuminated it just enough for him to make out the square of blue-gray liquid. Beyond that, the yard rose upward toward a tree-line along a distant, brick wall that curved out of sight.

"It's beautiful here. I'm happy for your success. That you have all of this. I have to say, I'm happy we met again. If we never see each other again, I will never forget this, all of this." He wanted to say *I will never forget you,* but stopped himself, fearing he was being too forward.

Kai sniffed as if irritated. "This place. It really is too big. Too much. But I had the money. I never had money before, not growing up, never. Not until a couple of years ago. I couldn't resist this place."

"Thank you for showing it to me. For bringing me out here."

"Yeah, fine. Whatever."

Dane walked around the edge of the pit where the grass was thickest and came up alongside the bench where Kai leaned back, legs crossed. He sat down next to him, placing his jacket in the space between them. He bowed his head until his chin almost touched his chest.

"Would you ever think—" Dane stopped, unable to finish.

"Think what?"

"Would you ever think of giving me a second chance?" As he spoke, he remembered the soft kiss, and how Kai had hesitated before scrambling away. Hesitated.

Kai sat very still. Almost as if he wasn't breathing.

Dane heard the crickets suddenly stop. The trees overhead whished and rattled in the wind.

Then he heard a strange sound and realized it was Kai. He was chuckling softly, then laughing. Dane lifted his head.

"You saying you want to date me?"

"I—yes—that's what I'm saying. If you want."

Kai laughed a little more, then said, "I don't ever date."

"Ever?"

Kai shook his head. "It's stupid."

"But you did it tonight. You bought the date."

"I did, didn't I? But I didn't think about it like a real date."

"Neither did I," Dane confessed.

"Like I said, I don't trust you."

"I know."

Kai leaned forward. His sleeves rode up his wrists. The dimness made his skin look dark, ghostly, soft.

"No," he said. "I won't date you."

Dane nodded, his whole body sagging in disappointment. His bangs had flown loose from the wind and dragged across his eyes. He was cold. He'd been rejected. Maybe now it really was time to go home.

He started to stand.

Kai reached out and placed his hand gently against Dane's upper arm. "I won't date you, but if you want to, you can come back inside the house. It's cold out here."

Dane did not know how to respond at first. In fact, he didn't believe he'd heard him right. But his body had heard. It tingled. He was shivering now, the cold air ruffling his hair again, going right through his thin shirt, but the suggestion that he might go back into that magnificent house and warm up sent a flame of excitement through him.

"All right, then," Dane said. He realized his voice was shaking.

Kai's hand fell away. They both stood at the same time.

"This doesn't mean I forgive you," Kai said huskily.

"Of course not." But Dane smiled into the shadows.

They went back over the odd-shaped stepping stones and down the rocky steps. The grass shimmered in silvery waves all about them.

The white of Kai's shirt glowed right in front of Dane, as if to pull him inward toward Kai's gravity, his energy. Kai walked quickly, nearly skipping down the steps, as if he had a force inside him that was brimming over. No wonder the man had succeeded so young in life at his business, his grand weather app company. He was fast, smart, unstoppable.

Dane tried to remember more of that day when Erik had ripped the boy's backpack, calling him names, literally terrifying him. Had Dane really just looked the other way? Yes. And there was a reason. Even then, he had seen the vibrancy of the boy, something under the surface that was light and heat and determination. And Erik was eviscerating it without a care, pushing that beauty down, ignorant of the gift of what was right in front of him flaming, pulsing behind that stringy hair, an ethereal beauty, an intelligence, a vital boy on the cusp of becoming a man.

Dane had turned away that day because he couldn't bear to see it. It was wrong. He knew that. But he couldn't look. And he couldn't stop it. And he didn't want to feel it happen because he didn't want to feel anything back then. The teen years had been so hard.

But now he remembered. He didn't want to see Kai beaten down. He didn't want to feel the hurt of that, or deal with it at all.

The man before him hopped onto the driveway, and his entire body, for a moment, was outlined in gold from the pole lamps and house lights. His hair drew the light in and shimmered and Dane could see every wisping strand like a precious softness he wanted to touch, to weave between his fingers.

When they reached the front door with the stained glass dragonflies, Kai opened it. Ben was nowhere in sight.

White light spilled onto the porch steps.

Kai nearly leaped inside.

Dane followed. As he crossed the threshold he had the thought: *I must remember this moment.* He was on the outside going in. Providing he handled things right, with this one step there would be a before and an after in his life, at least for this one night. With Kai.

As long as he didn't fuck it up again.

Part Two

The Seduction

*

Chapter Seven

Kai led them back to the living room with the colorful stone hearth and the long leather couch. Their abandoned wine glasses still stood on the coffee table, glittering in the dying firelight. The couch showed dents where they had been sitting. It was as if no time had passed.

Going straight toward the fireplace, Kai bent and tossed two logs onto the fire. The flames licked up in sunset brilliance, crackling loud. Scents of burning oak and leftover wine mixed on the air.

Dane could not help but watch the way Kai's body moved as he bent and flexed and turned. His hips were narrow and his ass looked slim and compact beneath the folds of his trousers. There was an energy to his movements that fizzed the air greater than the fire. His hands gripped the wood, strong and firm, but slim to match the rest of his build. His white shirt stretched across his chest as he stood, promising more hard leanness.

When Kai stood up he looked straight at Dane, who leaned against the arm of the couch, jacket still folded under his elbow. Kai's eyebrows narrowed, head tilted slightly to take the edge off the glare. Or maybe it wasn't a glare so much as a concentrated effort at hiding a resurgence of doubt.

Dane didn't dare breathe. Kai was like a feral thing at this moment, angry, skittish—and who could blame him? Dane had been his first crush, and had consorted with the enemy back in high school days.

With a grace that belied any nervousness, Kai strode to the coffee table, took up the wine and poured their glasses full. White for Dane. Red for Kai. As he set the second bottle down with a thunk, he said, quite calmly, "Aren't you going to sit?"

Dane moved quickly around the couch arm and sat, letting the cushions enfold his still shivering body. He leaned forward and picked up his wineglass. He lifted one leg up so his knee bent on the couch, foot trailing over the edge.

Kai came around the table, grabbed his own glass, and plunked himself hard in middle of the couch. It was a long sofa, so there were still several feet of space between them.

Kai's feet pressed flat to the black, plush rug. He took a sip of his wine, then rubbed the bottom of the glass below the stem back and forth over his right thigh. He looked straight ahead, the firelight awash in his hair and eyes.

Dane could not stop looking at him. He took a long sip of his own wine, feeling it heat him more than the fire. But neither the fire nor the wine warmed him more than the man who sat in front of him.

Finally, Kai leaned back and bent his own knee so that he sat facing Dane. The edge of his pant leg rode up revealing a black sock and a tiny strip of his lower shin. Dane's gaze was drawn to that, almost like a tease. Then his eyes traveled back up to the wrists, the throat and the warm skin just beneath, and finally that intriguing face from childhood, harder-edged now but no less beautiful for it.

Kai still glared. He brought his glass to his lips and drank, watching Dane over the shining rim.

Dane drank again, watching in return. Growing warmer.

The fire hissed and spat. The walls undulated with brown shadows.

The whole house was silent about them, except for this room and the rush of the fire. Except for Dane's own pulse which buzzed intermittently in his ears.

Each man took another drink. Then another. Their eyes stayed locked. It was uncanny and wonderful and scary and strange. Especially when Dane remembered he couldn't get Kai to look directly at him for most of the evening before he'd been thrown out. And in the dark, on their walk, there'd been little eye contact. Plus, they'd had dimness to keep their emotional vulnerabilities cloaked.

Dane let his lips part slightly after the last sip, knowing they were still a little damp. Counted on it.

Kai's eyebrows had relaxed now, giving him an almost sad expression. But his mouth was still drawn in, as if the wine was a little sour. The wine—or Dane?

Dane was still a little surprised this man was the same kid from junior high and high school. He saw the resemblance now, of course, but they were so far away from that time now. And yet, Kai was still so close to it. Teetering on the edge because he was still so bothered.

Dane had such an urge to gather him up into his arms. But the wilderness between them was still too great. He looked down, the first to glance off in many minutes, and saw his wine was half-gone. Kai had poured it full. His head began to spin a little in the most tender and delightful way.

Kai shook his head once, twice.

"I can't believe you didn't leave when I told you to," Kai said.

"I was upset."

Kai raised an eyebrow in silent question.

Dane continued, keeping his voice low. "I'm not used to staying where I'm not wanted. But I couldn't leave it like this between us. Even if you rejected me again, I had to see you one more time, to say… to…."

"To what? Apologize yet again?" He let out a huff of air. "A glutton for punishment?"

"No. But this time, now, well, I'm not some thoughtless kid anymore. I just wanted to make sure you're okay." Dane blinked, watching as a soft blush crawled up Kai's neck. He wanted to smile. Kai was taking him in, responding. This was nice, to actually see it even if Kai kept his eyes cool, his mouth tight.

"I guess," Dane said, "I just like to see things through, no T's uncrossed so to speak."

"You must just be nuts."

"I'm not the one who spent four grand for a date."

"For charity," Kai defended.

Were they going to go this round again? Over and over? It was getting old.

"For revenge," Dane offered, then immediately regretted it.

"No," Kai said with grave conviction.

Dane did not believe him, but it didn't matter. If Kai had brought him here for a confrontation, to make a point, Dane deserved it. He could live with that.

"Okay, then," Dane said, with a half-smile. "Because of the billboards."

Kai's glare lit up again.

"Hey, what?" Dane held one hand up in defense. He kept his wine glass tight against his thigh. "I'm proud of those ads."

Kai looked down, then up through dark lashes that softened the sharpness about him. Dane's heart contracted.

Kai breathed in, staring him down. He took another drink of his red wine. His Adam's apple moved up and down as he swallowed.

Everything was warm now. A little sleepy. Dreamy. Softly, Dane said, "Why'd you run from my kiss?"

Kai's eyebrows went up. He glanced toward the fire. "Who said I wanted you to kiss me?"

"No one. I wanted to."

Kai's eyes closed. He did not move for a long time, as if struggling inside himself with an unseen adversary. Maybe it was fear, or trust. Maybe something even deeper. Some need he did not wish to acknowledge.

"I wanted to," Dane repeated. Nervous again, he took another sip of wine.

Voice almost a whisper. "I thought you were just joking around."

"No. I wouldn't."

"I thought you were—that I was a fool—that I am a fool for bringing you here."

"I don't think that," Dane argued. "I don't think that at all."

"Why not? I brought you here to remind you of a past we both seem wary of. I had no other motive."

Perhaps no conscious motive, Dane thought.

Aloud, he said, "Nothing about you is foolish in my eyes. That's what I think. Maybe that's why I stuck around tonight. To make sure you know that."

"Everything you say—it's as if you're trying to get on my good side. Maybe I don't have a good side."

Dane laughed openly.

"What's so funny?" Kai asked.

"Nothing. You may think you don't have a good side. Well, then, okay. But you're awesome." His blood pounded at his own words. Kai made him feel awesome, even with all the rejection, that much was true.

"You don't even know me."

Dane shrugged. "I know enough. I tried to kiss you because of it. No other reason, no jokes, nothing like that."

Kai let out a sound of disbelief.

Dane scoffed. "If you weren't so skittish and flippant, I'd do it again."

"Now you're insulting me?"

"Just an observation." Dane smiled. This was torture. And kind of fun. A turn on every time Kai rebuffed him. He didn't want to know why. He just liked it.

"I'm not skittish."

Dane tilted his head down, looking at his wine and the firelight dancing in it. "All right, then." He leaned sideways and set his wine on the coffee table. It wobbled a little. His hand was shaking. Then he scooted forward on the couch, watching as "not skittish" Kai swayed back.

Dane reached out and took the wine glass from Kai's hand, setting it next to his own. He let his hand fall, lightly touching Kai on the knee. He felt the muscles there flinch as Kai fought to hold still. His fingertips felt as if they were burning.

Kai's brow went tight again, eyes squinting as he looked at him. "You think I'm a fool."

"I don't. Honest." Dane's heart pounded even harder.

"Then do it. Just do it."

Those words, so harsh, un-sexy. As if Kai was asking Dane to take out the trash. He wasn't so easily put off.

Dane had to lean pretty far to reach Kai, who wasn't making things easy by still leaning back, eying him as if he had turned into a ghoul. He held his breath and brushed his lips across Kai's. Soft plumpness. Wine and spice. Hardly any pressure. A subtle warmth suffusing through his body. He pulled back a few inches to see Kai's eyes avoiding him, looking to the left, then up.

"That's it?" Kai asked the wall.

Dane bit his lower lip. His stomach clenched. "It's a start."

Kai drew in a deep breath. "Do it again."

Dane held back a smile and leaned in, fingertips lightly resting on Kai's knee. He wanted to move his hands up to Kai's waist or shoulders, take him into a light embrace. But for the moment the risk was too great. Kai was poised to bolt.

This time the kiss lasted longer, the pressure more intense. Their mouths stayed closed, but excitement surged through Dane's body.

When he pulled back again, cool green eyes met his gaze. Dane held still, as if facing a wild animal, watching as Kai's hand came up to his face, almost touching Dane's cheek. Kai pulled back, lips curling down.

"Don't fuck with me."

"I'm not," Dane whispered.

"Because—because you can't just—you can't do it like that, kiss like that and be just fucking around."

The words sparked his blood. Kai had liked the kiss. And Dane had barely done much.

"I'm not," Dane repeated.

Kai sat up straight, cool and unruffled. But his hand was fisted at his thigh.

Dane's fingers touched air now. He missed the contact of that knee.

"Give me a minute," Kai said.

Dane nodded as Kai turned away.

Finally, Kai spoke. "It can't go like that. It can't."

"What can't?"

"This."

"A date?" Dane asked.

"No. *This* date."

Dane clasped his hands together. They were still shaking. "This date can be whatever you want it to be."

"Why? Because I paid for it?"

"No. Because I am giving my permission. Not because you paid." Dane took a deep breath. "And if you tell me to leave again, then this time I will. But, Kai, I don't really want to leave."

Kai's eyes were bright, glittered with distrust. "You see me now, don't you? When it's convenient."

"What?"

"Now that I'm tall, nicely dressed, wealthy. You see me now, don't you?"

Dane nodded, but a slow disappointment sent a coldness into him, threatening to put out the heat in his body, his lovely reaction to Kai.

"But you didn't see me that day. You looked away. I wasn't enough to be part of your world."

A log in the fireplace fell, sending up vivid sparks of coppery orange. Dane closed his eyes and saw the same colors on the backs of his eyelids. He had stayed. Even when he wasn't wanted. Why?

"I saw you that day. I did. Yes, you had to remind me, but I saw you. I have no excuses about turning away. I just did. A powerless feeling—"

"Powerless? Back then you had everything. Erik who ran the fucking school. Your looks. You still have everything. You were never powerless."

He was wrong, but he was right at the same time.

Kai said, "You don't know what it's like. To be invisible. I hope you never do. I'm not trying to whine. I'm making a point. You're fucking beautiful and you've never lived a day not being so."

Beauty. It had been a thing. Yes. Adults pinched Dane's cheeks when he was a toddler. He never went through an awkward stage. Girls smiled at him everywhere. Some people sang, or painted, or played musical instruments. Dane was good at turning heads. Kai never sent him love notes in high school, but he had received a lot of them from kids, and he'd ignored them.

He got attention. He was seen. He made it work for himself. In drama classes. And with his first modeling job which he got on only his first audition. That sort of thing rarely happened to anyone.

But when the day was done and all he had was himself, he would sit and think about how meaningless it was. He didn't create anything. He used his own looks to be that guy selling that product, but in the end the art of it was done by everyone else. He had his moments of pride, sure, but they were fleeting. He would lose his looks one day and then what would he have?

"Visibility can be fleeting." Dane said his thought out loud. "It comes and goes. I'll get older and no one will want me. Unless there's something more. So you want to talk to me about that? About my fucking beauty? Okay. But you're not so bad yourself. You have to know that. And you've created something out of nothing. Can't say I've done the same for myself." He offered a wry smile.

"Companies can be fleeting. Wealth like mine can be fleeting."

"So you understand, then."

"Yeah, but you don't, yet. You don't at all."

"I'll tell you something," Dane said, stretching back on the side of the couch. "I'm not visible. I have this mask on. And no one sees beyond it. I don't get credit for what's beneath. No one cares. Not in school. Not in my current line of work. So maybe I do get it."

"I never got you out of my mind." Kai smirked. "Like poison there."

Dane's heart sped up to hear it. He wanted to kiss him again. And again. How could he make Kai believe that?

"So now I'm here. And we're on a date. What could be bad about that?"

Kai said, "Maybe everything."

"I liked kissing you."

Kai put a hand to his lips. "Did you know you were gay back then? At fifteen?"

Dane shook his head. "I told you before that I didn't." There had been too many things in his teen years he had refused to face.

"I did," Kai said. "Another reason to hide. To be invisible."

"It does make things harder." How lonely Kai must have been, Dane thought.

"Why didn't you tell the charity that you were gay? That you wanted to be auctioned off for a gay date? Why are you not publicly out?"

"I'm just not. I don't hide it either, but with the charity I didn't want to over-complicate matters."

"I see." Kai picked up his wine and drank.

"Maybe you think I'm wrong for not being out, but—"

"No," Kai interrupted. "It's the easier road for some."

"People who know me know I'm out. And I have dated women. It's no big deal to me. So I figured for charity, for one night and a dinner out I'd be fine. I expected female bidders."

"And here you are."

"Yes. Not what I expected."

"Yeah, you snagged an asshole for a date."

Dane raised his eyebrows. "That's not what I think."

What he thought was that he was becoming more and more attracted to Kai. Had been the entire evening. Kai was scarred, wary, untrusting, but not an asshole.

All Kai said was, "Hmm."

For awhile they sat, the fire crackling, the room soft and warm, as if it was conducive to keeping secrets.

Blurted out, under his breath, Kai said, "You're so god damn beautiful. I don't know what to do with that."

After everything he'd just thought and said about fleeting beauty, its emptiness, Kai's admission, his sudden trust – enough to give this compliment—gave Dane a rush of arousal. This moment was precious and Dane was not going to take it for granted. "You don't have to do anything, just try to believe me when I say you're—you're—"

"What?"

"Really hot. And I wanted to kiss you. Both times. And I want to do it again."

Kai set his wine glass down again.

Some guys didn't ever kiss when they hooked up, saying it was too intimate. Yet they could invade each other's bodies in other ways and go home intoxicated on orgasms and be on the prowl by the next week. They were looking for the drug of sex and nothing more permanent. The more beautiful you were in the gay community, the more that sort of behavior was expected.

But not Dane. He had had only three short-term boyfriends. Hook ups that lead to no commitments, one of which had led to dating. That guy had slept with other guys while dating Dane. Kai was not the only one with trust issues.

Dane liked kissing. Apparently that wasn't a big thing with prowling men. But he wanted to do it before he got to the other stuff, which involved touching and holding and revealing of body parts in engorged states which always made him tremble a little. He always closed his eyes when he came.

He wasn't ashamed of sex, or being gay, it was simply that the act made him feel so damned vulnerable. He had tried to pick partners who were gentler, nicer, and they were rarer than he'd expected to encounter in his dealings. Most were wild-natured, crass, hard partiers.

Kai did not seem nicer, and truly Dane knew very little about him so far, but he seemed more like Dane: wanting something more, wanting meaning. He had liked kissing him because Kai hadn't grabbed him. Because Kai had let him do it soft and didn't laugh or tease him for it. The kiss had filled him with a longing that made him want another kiss. And touching as well. Desire flared in him. For Kai. With Kai. Imagining himself in Kai's arms.

No, Kai was right, this was not the date he'd expected tonight. This was so much better.

Chapter Eight

There was a yearning in Kai's eyes Dane was sure he was not misreading. He leaned in for a third—or was it the fourth?—kiss.

Their lips met and Dane's body immediately surged with arousal. When he'd kissed men before, it had felt okay but not like this. Not like this roller coaster ride where his stomach flopped over and over at the fast curves and swift descents.

For the first time, Kai touched him, raising his hand slowly and brushing the side of his head with his fingertips.

Dane parted his lips to catch more of Kai's mouth in a deeper pull. He felt the other man tremble against his mouth. He put his hand on Kai's shoulder.

Everything had to be slow at first. All of it. Kai needed to be handled like a valuable possession. With care. Reverence.

Or so he thought.

Kai's hand on his face moved until the edge of his palm rested against Dane's cheek. His other hand came up and bumped Dane's arm, moving under his shoulder. He felt fingers grip the cloth against his upper back.

The leather of the couch made it easy to scoot forward and the space between them shrank. Everything spun in a dizzy rapture. Dane could not recall when the kiss had graduated from a light touch to an embrace, their chests pressing.

Kai was warm in his arms, his chest rising and falling against Dane's, his arms tightening. Dane wanted this more than anything in his life up to now. The breath of this glowering man. That resentful, vibrant heartbeat matched to his.

When he pulled back for a breath, there was gold in Kai's eyes. Kai's bangs were loose and brushing Dane's brow.

Kai tasted of fire, and the citrus of his sleek, red wine.

Dane leaned in for more. The next kiss lasted longer, went deeper.

He could not say who pulled back first. They were facing each other, eyes half-closed, breaths coming fast and hard. Kai's teeth were gritted, his mouth set in a line of fierce concentration. Kai's left hand rested, still half-gripping against Dane's side. Dane's left hand cupped Kai's shoulder. To a bystander, they might have been poised for a fight. But fighting Kai was the last thing on Dane's mind.

Kai took a deep, shaky breath. His left eyebrow twitched. He was beautiful.

"Maybe," Kai said in a rough voice, "it's time to give you a tour of this gargantuan excuse for a home."

"All right." Dane's words sounded faraway. At this moment, he'd follow Kai to hell if Kai asked him to.

Kai took his hand away from Dane's side and pushed himself up to stand. He wobbled a bit, and Dane liked that he'd put the man off-kilter. Maybe that was why Kai stopped for the moment. Maybe it was going too far too fast.

When Kai got his balance, he looked down at Dane with glittering eyes. Then he reached out his hand in offering.

Dane took it, feeling the grip, clenching in return, and Kai pulled him forward as Dane stood on rather unsteady legs.

"Bring your wine along if you'd like," Kai said huskily.

Their hands were still clasped. Dane grabbed his glass in his free hand and followed Kai around the couch, stepping off the plush rug and onto the hard, marble floor.

They came to the door of the living room. Kai opened it, still drawing Dane forward with his hand. Dane delighted in it. Holding hands. So sweet. And not something he'd done before with other guys.

Kai did not seem fazed by it in the least, pulling Dane into the room with the twin staircases.

As if talking about the weather—or weather apps—Kai said, "This place is pretty big. You've seen the dining room. There is another living room down here but I don't use it. Off that room is a large bed and bath and Ben lives there most of the time. He sorta came with the place. I liked him so I kept him on."

A house that comes with its own butler, Dane thought. *Like a fairytale.*

"The upstairs is divided into two huge suites. Each with its own stairway. I live in the suite to the right."

Dane gulped. "To the right, then?"

"You don't have to." Kai looked unsure, though his cheeks still held color from their kisses.

"You're just giving me a tour, right?"

Kai let out a sound of disgust. "Right."

Dane smiled, and clutched Kai's hand tighter to show he was up for more than a tour. If that was what Kai wanted. "Show me."

Kai's lips twitched. Dane wondered what a real smile from them would look like. He hoped he'd find out before the end of the night.

The stairs were rough white marble threaded with black swirls. The curving banister was polished wood, a deep nut brown, and carved with sweeping waves, as if the material itself held an inner tide waiting to be released.

Kai took the stairs quickly, each step a quick stride-hop, and Dane hurried to keep up, not wanting to let go of that warm, wonderful hand he held.

At the top, he spared a glance down at the gleaming floor they'd just left, and the foyer beyond. It was only moments ago he had been on the other side of those glass front doors, agonizing that he'd never be invited back inside.

The landing was as huge as a bedroom itself, the floor decorated with a huge black and white checkered rug. There was a blue-tinged square mirror on one wall. Beyond, a white-walled hall beckoned.

Opposite the mirror stood a side table with a lamp with stained glass shaped into more dragonflies. Did Kai like dragonflies, or had that come with the house like the butler did?

The lamp cast pink and blue shadows on the pale wall. Pretty.

Everything about this place was wonderful. Including Kai. Dane wanted to tell him that, but the words stuck in the back of his throat.

"I haven't done much with the furnishings here, but follow me," Kai said. He still wasn't smiling, but his words belied a hint of pride. Maybe some urgency, too.

"Don't worry. I'm already impressed beyond words."

"Hmph," was all Kai said.

Making their way down the hall, the two came into a wide, long room with windows all along one side, draped elegantly with silvery gray drapes. The room had a small alcove near the entryway, where a desk and computer sat. The computer was on, humming to itself. Along the single alcove wall that separated it from the bedroom was a huge bookshelf filled with notebooks, books and knickknacks.

The entire floor was black. Within the room, a huge bed with a white comforter took center stage. It was piled with different sized pillows. It had a bench at the foot, lined with beige cushions, centered on a small gray rug. There was a low lacquer-black bureau attached to a high dresser. Along the low section sat a plain, white lamp, a stack of thick books that looked like texts, and a couple of boxes—jewelry boxes, Dane guessed.

The tall ceiling curved in the middle. The room smelled of soap and lemon, as if it had recently been cleaned.

Everything about the room was elegant and angular, like Kai, but darker, filled with shadows to hide in.

Dane wanted to see Kai swathed in flaxen colors: amber, cream, caramel. But this room was intriguing, spare and masculine, if a little cool.

The white bed with the black base, however, looked sumptuous, comfortable. He might sink into it with a lover and never want to come back up for air.

Kai pulled his hand away from Dane's, sudden, as if being in his own room and holding a man's hand at the same time was too much for him.

"There's a full closet in there." He pointed at two glass doors at one end. "Like a whole other room. And a bath with separate shower… huge. And a balcony off the back. There's a fridge out there, and a sink. You could hold barbecues in this bedroom and balcony alone, invite the family, everything."

Dane grinned. "Really?"

Still no smile. But Kai did manage a swift head-tilt, acknowledging his own decadence.

"There are buttons you can push in the closet that bring your clothes right up to you on the hangar, showing you what you have, offering more if you decline. Same for the shoe rack."

"Gadgets," Dane stated.

"Exactly."

Will he smile now? Dane wondered. *What if I sprinkled him with gadgets? If I made myself a gadget for his well-being…*

He laughed at himself. He was willing to do anything it took now to land this man, to call him *his*.

"I love it," Dane said. He turned all the way around. "It's awesome."

"I came a long way from that kid with the torn backpack taking Erik's threats."

Dane looked down, still ashamed. "We both have."

"He hit me once, you know."

"What?" Dane did *not* recall that.

"You were there but you didn't see it. You had your back to him. I'd been watching you, I guess." He swept his hand through the air as if to brush away an irritant. "He caught me. You never knew I watched you, but he did. It enraged him. I almost thought *he* had a thing for you. You were talking to some guys and Erik wandered over to me and just decked me. Right on the chin. I went backward, arms all out, landing hard on my ass. People were all around. Some of them laughed. You didn't hear it. You were in your own world."

"All through high school I was in my own world. It was self-preservation."

"I know that."

"That's awful, what he did. Everything Erik did. I am sorry I didn't notice."

Kai turned away and walked toward the lacquer dresser, running a hand along one smooth edge. Dane took one step forward. Stopped. Panic scraped the insides of his belly. He couldn't lose him now. If Kai put his barriers back up and pushed him out, Dane might sit down and start to howl.

Such a fine line Kai cut as he walked. Self-assured. Confident. But underneath he was so tentative. That shy kid was still close. The memories of ten, nine and eight years ago not yet blurred.

Dane moved forward again, touching Kai on the center of his back, lightly, oh so gently.

"Show me the closet. I want to see the gadgets."

Kai turned. He eyed Dane up and down. His pink lips made a tight line. The pupils of his eyes were wide, a depthless black from which this man gazed at him so intently.

"Maybe later," Kai said.

"All right." Dane blinked twice. Let his lips part, curve up a little. He knew he could beckon with very little effort. He didn't do it as a game, though, not with anyone outside of photo shoots, and he never wanted to do that with Kai.

Kai's mouth twisted. He breathed in through his nose with a hiss.

"Fuck!" Kai reached out and grabbed him by the upper arms, bringing Dane close. This time he initiated the kiss, and it was not a simple, gradual touch. Not light. And yet when their mouths met, this time they both opened. The first tentative touch of tongues was so tender Dane's body and mind swooned.

Dane reached up and placed his hand at the back of Kai's neck, pulling him closer.

Kai found the collar of Dane's shirt and dug his fingers inside it, dragging them along his nape. Tingles like electricity coursed through Dane's body. This man was hot. He was everything Dane could want in his arms, smart, well-educated, and he smelled good. Like spice and wine. He was making out with an autumn tycoon, sovereign of this little hill in the middle of the easternmost suburbs of L.A.

This was really happening. All because of an auction and a strange bid from a mysterious man in a hoodie.

This was turning into a great night.

It didn't seem possible, but the kiss intensified as their mouths opened further as if to suck each other in. Dane moved his hands up and down Kai's back, exploring the hard muscle and bone tapering to the waist, daring to press the small of the back, pinky finger brushing slightly lower.

Finally, Kai turned until his lips pressed only the side of Dane's mouth. His cheek rubbed against his chin, then moved up and he could feel Kai's breath against his ear.

"I can't believe you're here."

"I am," Dane replied.

"Do you need—do you want to leave now?"

"Do you want me to?"

"Not right now."

The answer sounded unhopeful, but the tone of voice was not cruel. It surrounded Dane with a silkiness, a rawness of desire for this man who had just now stolen his breath.

They held each other close, jaws rubbing. Kai's body trembled just under the surface of his skin.

Dane took the lead now.

"That bed looks like the softest I've ever seen."

"It is." Another tremor. A harder clutch at Dane's nape.

"I feel like I need to sit before I fall."

"Okay," Kai said.

Dane backed up, avoiding the foot bench, until the backs of his legs hit the side of the bed. Kai took the opportunity to his advantage and gave a little shove. Dane sat, bouncing a little. The bed was incredible. He could easily imagine himself lounging naked in it. Kai beside him.

Kai's hands were on his shoulders, pushing until Dane fell all the way back, face up, and Kai crawled over him, straddling his hips.

All right, then. It was going to happen and Dane could not think of anything he wanted more. He reached up and pulled Kai down on top of him, wanting to feel his weight. It was like holding all bone and sinew. Kai felt wiry, hard. Certainly this was proof he did not spend all his time in an office.

Their lips met again. Kai was a great kisser. Dane had to close his eyes against the intensity, taking it all in while still trying to keep some control.

He held a man in his arms who had been a frightened, diminished kid, and now he had power, he had everything, and Dane was holding him, caressing him, kissing him.

Dane pulled back this time, pressing their cheeks together. "I want you closer."

Kai pushed up on one arm. His other hand came up and tugged at the buttons of Dane's shirt. Dane reached up between Kai's arms and began undoing Kai's buttons, revealing a lot of tanned flesh as he pushed the edges of the shirt apart.

Kai could not undo Dane's buttons one-handed, so when Dane was finished, he reached for his own shirt. Kai took that moment to sit up and shrug out of his, leaving himself bare and gleaming in the low white light of the room.

His chest was flat, not overly muscular, but well-formed. He had glints of golden hair in the very center, dusting toward the nipples and then vanishing entirely. His ribs dented his skin in subtle ripples, tapering to a slim waist and flat stomach. His bellybutton was a shallow, beckoning oval of thin shadow.

Dane struggled to loosen his arms from his shirt.

Kai, looking down at him, chuckled and seemed to take pity, for he reached out and tugged each sleeve free of Dane's arms, pulling as Dane lifted his upper body. When Dane's shirt was free, Kai tossed it to the side and Dane could hear it land in a quiet hush on the hard, black floor.

Kai looked down at him again, gave a small gasp, and came forward, pressing his hand flat against Dane's chest, making a half-circle before stopping just over his heart.

Dane slid his hands around that waist, feeling the softness of the skin and the flexing of the muscles beneath it. Kai was very warm, smooth and hard at the same time, and touching him felt insanely wonderful. He wanted to feel his skin against Kai's. Skin on skin. That was all he could think at the moment. He was so aroused it made him dizzy. That and maybe a tad too much wine.

But in this moment the room became a haven, a closed space of safety and private desire, and it was warm, so warm, despite the austere coldness of its décor.

Kai let up. He looked at Dane with an almost pained look, and made a sound of utter desperation. Adoration. Dane smiled, endeared even more by the thought that Kai had wanted him for a long, long time. Kai gave another groan. He leaned up and cupped Dane's cheek. The way he gazed at Dane was more intimate than the kiss.

Dane's cock, half-hard, now filled all the way and he let out an answering moan. The plush comforter almost absorbed him as Kai pushed closer, rubbing against his crotch. There was an answering firmness.

"I want you," Dane said.

Kai's hand trailed across Dane's chest to his waistband. Dane tilted his head up, undoing the clasp and wriggling as both of them pushed his trousers, along with his underwear, all the way down. He toed off his shoes and the pants came all the way off. Kai slid away from him, standing before him, bare-chested and gleaming. He bent and took Dane's socks off and now Dane lay fully naked before him.

The white comforter was like waves of foam, soft against his skin. He knew he looked good and was proud of it, even if it was shallow. His looks had attracted Kai to him in the first place, hadn't they? He wasn't the only shallow one here. And yet, there was something more. This didn't feel like a normal hook up. For one thing, the excitement in his mind and body superseded mere physical arousal. There had been vulnerabilities shared between them this evening that were about more than unclothed skin and flushed body parts. A deeper connection. Did Kai feel it, too? Dane bit his lower lip, trying not to hope too much. As long as Kai followed through with this evening and made love to him, Dane would allow himself to be happy about it. He would let him call him "vapid" all he wanted. If only he would touch him…

His cock ached where it arched against his abdomen, already wet at the tip. He took a deep breath as Kai straightened and looked down at him, grazing his body with a tender look.

Dane's stomach fluttered.

"You're unbelievable," Kai muttered, almost in disgust.

Dane smiled wide and scooted back on the bed. He held out his arms.

Kai undid his own trousers, hopped a bit to get out of his shoes, and when everything was shucked and he was naked, he slid alongside Dane.

His cock was golden, pink at the head and so pretty and hard. It stood straight out from his body. When Kai lay down, that cock nuzzled Dane's thigh before settling against his own hardness as they moved into each other's arms.

It had been a long while since Dane had had sex with anyone other than himself. It felt good to hold another person, a young and beautiful man who wanted him as deeply as he wanted in return.

Dane reached up and embraced Kai's head, bringing him in for another kiss. This time his body was allowed to feel it all, as if the kiss itself went all over him inside and out.

Their tongues traced the delicate, soft insides of their mouths. It was like being fully taken by that very simple, close gesture, and Dane undulated against Kai, feeling him tremble again. Their bodies made small thrusts against each other that sent explosions of arousal stinging through Dane's body over and over.

He wondered how long he could keep this up before he would explode into a million pieces scattered about the black and white room.

He pulled away. "I can't last like this. It's—you're—so—"

"What?" Kai asked.

"You're fantastic." The silken touch of Kai's skin against his mouth, hands, body. The way Kai's leg moved smoothly over his thigh, almost possessive. The sweet, addicting taste of him. The warmth growing to a conflagration of unchecked desire.

Kai moved over Dane, putting both hands on either side of his head. His body lay on top of him now, chest to chest, belly to belly, cock to cock. He still wasn't smiling.

"You don't have to last," Kai said softly.

Dane swallowed hard. "I want it to last."

"I'm not going to kick you out on your ass again, if that's what you're worried about. Unless you fail to please me." Now there was a small curve of the upper lip, but a smirk more than a smile.

Dane laughed out loud.

"So don't hold back," Kai commanded.

Kai leaned down and nuzzled Dane's neck, licking, kissing, and Dane's cock twitched between them.

Like the genius he was at everything he did, Kai made love to him slowly, lavishing attention to his neck, shoulders, chest. When he reached Dane's nipples he licked and sucked until they were hard as pebbles on the cool air.

He traveled further down, kissing as he went, along ribs and tummy, laving a wet path about his bellybutton, leaving Dane gasping, and his cock nearly in pain, ready to burst.

Dane cried out when Kai reached his thighs, placing kisses all along the insides. Shamelessly, Dane's legs spread for him.

Finally, Kai's breath puffed against his taut balls. A desperation rose up in him, and a sweetness he knew to be associated with sex, but something more, too, a pureness opening inside him. This man more than intrigued him. He was like someone from a wakening dream-fantasy of the best sex companion he could imagine. Someone he wanted even more, someone to trust, to cling to, to confess all his secrets and inner thoughts to.

A wet, hot tongue lapped at Dane's balls. His cock throbbed in ecstasy. He cried out again. Heard himself begging, as if from faraway. "Please. Please."

Finally, the tongue reached the root of him; it slowly licked up, soft and strong at the same time, and his cock twitched up and rocked as if seeking its master.

"Please," he begged one more time.

Kai was good. So good. He brought his mouth upward and let his tongue touch the crown of Dane's cock, tickling with quick flicks. Lapping the slit. Dane had never felt so overcome.

He said, "I'm not going to last."

Like a nightmare, the mouth went away. "It's all right," came the soothing response.

But it wasn't. He needed Kai now. So much. He was melting in his grip, his embrace, and there was nothing left of him but the agonizing desire threatening to devour him.

His body shook as hands clutched the bedspread on either side of his hips. Then he felt it, the heat of breath first, the lap of tongue, and pliant, strong lips suctioning over his tip and moving down.

Everything inside him rushed to be at that center of being, his body a stretched tight figure of flesh and blood and bone waiting to break.

Kai went down, then up, then down again taking him further into his mouth, slick and strong. The sucking strengthened and oh it was good, so good, he could be devoured and never see light or air or life again and it would all be good if Kai would just keep that up, never stop. Never stop.

He wanted to reach up and pull that head down further, but he still had some semblance of the polite man he'd been raised to be. Instead, he gripped the thick comforter with his fingers until he thought it would tear, bucking up.

"So good. Oh god… I can't hold it. I can't!"

Kai sucked harder, his hand coming away from Dane's hip to grip him tightly about the base of his cock, encouraging, milking as he suckled.

Dane gave a strangled moan. Fire raged through him from the back of his head to his spine, to his balls, to the tips of his toes.

His cock jerked and he felt himself go up and up into white snowy blankness peppered with sparks of red and green before spilling over into the euphoric ocean of orgasm.

He felt himself spurting into Kai's mouth over and over, and his cock felt strong and hard as it continued to spasm even after Kai had sucked him dry.

This was different. This was better. This was the best he'd ever had. And for a moment he didn't wonder about that, but let himself lie back contented, basking in the way Kai's tongue softly comforted his wilting cock.

Kai crawled over him again, kissing him, and Dane's arms went around his shoulders. Kai's cock nudged his abdomen. Dane rolled them until Kai was on his back, and ran his hand over his smooth chest and belly.

Kai's knees bent a little and he tossed his head from side to side as Dane caressed his sides, hips and thighs. When his fingers curled around Kai's stiffness, Kai gasped.

Dane smiled, watching his face closely, looking for any smile in return. Still nothing. But Kai's face was softened in bliss, his eyes half-closed, the lashes making small feathered shadows against the tops of his cheeks.

Dane leaned down and licked Kai's cock all over. The body beneath him rocked. The hips bucked as Dane took the head into his mouth and teased it with his tongue.

The room filled with sounds of euphoria.

Dane lowered his mouth as far down as was comfortable and began to slide his lips up and down the length, swiping his tongue over the tip as he came up, sucking harder on his way down.

It wasn't long before Dane was rewarded with insistent throbs, and a nearly sobbing man coming in his mouth.

Breathless, he released the softening cock, petting it, then cupping it with his warm hand as he came up in the bed and took Kai into his arms.

Kai was still catching his breath, looking at him sidelong as if he thought Dane might vanish like a dream. Kai caught him up and held tight, still shuddering in afterglow.

Dane felt bold now. He said, "I'll be wanting to do that again."

Kai murmured into his shoulder. "Sometimes you have to do things twice to make sure."

Dane chuckled. "Agreed."

It might take some time to melt this guy, but Dane was up for the challenge.

Dane closed his eyes. Holding Kai against him was like holding something bright and light, not heavy, as if they fit together by some unknown law newly discovered.

Propped against elegant pillows, Dane saw Kai wave his hand and the lights dimmed to semi-darkness. Dane closed his eyes as Kai's warm breath brushed over his forehead.

Chapter Nine

For a long while Dane dozed, not realizing he was actually falling asleep.

He woke to hushed darkness. His left arm was numb where Kai lay on it. He pulled away gently, not wanting to disturb him. Kai moved with a soft shush of skin against the comforter but did not wake. His breathing remained slow and even.

Dane got up, looking down at his naked lover, realizing the room had gotten slightly chilled. He took the edge of the comforter that dragged the floor and folded it over Kai.

He found his way to the shadowed bathroom, which was some kind of shrine to bodily functions with a toilet like a throne and a shower of natural rock with five large spigots that could easily produce a waterfall.

When Dane found his way back to the bedroom, Kai was sitting up in bed, a frozen silhouette, the comforter making white waves about his waist.

"Where'd you go?" he asked.

Dane pressed his bare knees against the side of the bed, looking down at him. "I had to pee."

"I thought—I thought—"

Dane frowned. Kai was shaking.

Dane tried not to wonder about too many things at once, like what in the hell was going to happen after tonight.

"Hey. I didn't leave. I wouldn't do that to you right now. I didn't do that even when you tossed me out."

"I'm still not sure I understand why." Kai was looking at his lap. Dane saw in the dimness his fingers clench and unclench.

Second thoughts?

Dane shivered and knelt on the bed before him, boldly gathering him into his arms. "You're not sure? After—after what we did?"

Kai shook his head and did not embrace him in return.

Dane pressed his lips to his forehead, still and chaste, brushing the pale hair back from his face. "Seriously?"

He felt Kai's chest expand as he took a deep breath.

"Then," Dane said, "I guess I need to up my game."

One of Kai's arms came up to touch his naked waist. "Do what?"

"Try harder. Do better."

"You want to do this again?" Kai asked.

Did Kai mean now, or after tonight? Covering both prospects, he answered. "I said I want that, didn't I?"

Vague shapes surrounded them in their midnight forms. Shades of curtains, bureau shadows, a leather chair. If Dane concentrated hard enough, he could hear the whisper-soft hum of the computer in the alcove. There was a waver on the air as Kai shifted in his arms, cheek still pressed to the top of Dane's shoulder. Kai's hair smelled of October.

"I never thought—" Kai began.

Dane could hear the hurt in that tone and felt somehow responsible. "Kai. Kai, I see you."

Kai nodded against him.

"Kai, I see you. And you're beautiful."

"Then stay."

"Okay."

"And definitely up your game."

Dane winced. He couldn't tell from Kai's tone if he was being sarcastic or critical. He would not take it to heart. He had heard the man cry out in ecstasy only a short time ago. He'd done everything right.

He placed his hand under Kai's chin and tilted his head up, kissing him. When Dane pulled back, Kai was breathless. Yes, that last statement had to be sarcasm.

106

"I will do my best," Dane said, hoping Kai could see his smile through the dimness.

Dane rearranged the pillows, and pulled the comforter up until they were both beneath it.

He did not know this man well enough to read him yet. It scared him, but it also forced him to be brave. He draped his arm over Kai's back, and pushed his other arm beneath him and around his ribs. The embrace pulled Kai forward and Kai pressed his whole body against the front of Dane's, giving a shuddering gasp. Dane turned and kissed him on the cheek.

"You're shaking. What am I going to do with you?"

Kai put his arms around Dane's waist. Heat poured out between them from chest to groin, stirring them both. Dane's cock poked Kai's hip. Kai's erection thickened against Dane's thigh.

Temperatures rose.

Dane pushed his knee between Kai's legs, bringing them closer, then kissed Kai again on the lips, mouth wide open, demanding. He felt Kai's hand snake up over his chest, graze a nipple, and move up to cup the back of his head and pull him closer.

Dane smiled into the kiss, making it sweeter for them both, deeper. It wasn't enough. His hands roamed over Kai's back and sides, hips and buttocks, touching him everywhere he could reach, feeling the skin grow tense and feverish where he touched.

Kai arched in his arms, lowering his head to Dane's neck, latching on with a gentle bite as he tried to hold back his gasps and moans. They didn't speak, save a few "yeses" and an occasional "hell, fuck and damn."

Kai's lips found his again, and the passion—for there couldn't be any other word for it—rose to dizzying heights. Lightheaded, Dane could only focus now on two things. The man in his arms. And his cock that responded so readily to him.

Dane forced Kai back and began to lick and kiss his way all over the man's body. His hand found just enough space to wiggle between Kai's legs and curl around the burning hardness there, already slick at the tip, and hot, so hot. Everything was fire encased in shadow, greedy and blooming about them, and the comforter ended up at the foot of the bed in a wrinkled, cast-off, satin heap.

Dane scooted down some more and licked Kai's cock, up and down, and saw Kai's arms raise about his head, grabbing at air, then finally finding a pillow and pulling it over his face as he yelled and thrust at Dane's face.

Taking pity, Dane drew the tip into his mouth and sucked down. Then Kai was thrusting more, faster and harder. Dane kept himself still, wanting him to have his way, glorying in the revelation that he could break this man open like this, force him to lose control.

The taste of Kai grew spiced and cloying in his mouth. The pre-cum grew saltier. He knew Kai was seconds away now, and sucked harder.

Kai's legs came off the bed, then down as his hips bucked. His hands pounded the pillow, which flew off the side of the bed into the dark unknown, and he let loose a cry so sharp and aching that Dane himself nearly came to hear it.

He swallowed every hot spurt Kai had to give.

As soon as he pulled free of Kai's cock, Dane came up and wrapped Kai in his arms. Kai's hands clutched at his shoulders and he hissed into Dane's chest, the side of his face damp against his right nipple.

He held Kai still until the man regained some control.

Dane was still so close. As Kai moved back a little, the tip of Dane's cock grazed the man's bony hip and he thought he was going to lose it and come right then. His breaths came faster.

Kai seemed to understand his state and pushed him onto his back, running his hands up and down his chest. Then he raised one hand and touched his cheek, softly stroking, and leaned in. This time the kiss was a flutter against his lips. Kai's warm breath washed over him. His mouth slid along his jaw to his neck and licked.

Kai said, "I think I can't get enough of you."

The room spun. The words alone nearly undid him. Dane bit his lip hard, trying to hold back, to prolong this moment.

Kai's hands moved downward again, his mouth following along the center of his chest, sternum, and stomach. His head bowed and firm lips lowered over Dane's cock.

Dane held his hips down, vowing not to slam into Kai's face. He reached out with his hands, tried to grab a shoulder or a hand... anything, but his arms flailed on the air as if he were struggling not to drown. But he was drowning. He had hardly any breath left.

A firm palm stroked up as a strong mouth sucked down.

Dane heard a whimper. Himself. "I can't—I can't breathe." As his voice trembled up through his throat, his body twisted; he sat up and grabbed Kai's shoulders in a half-embrace and shot into his mouth.

He was still shaking all over when Kai's body lifted and Kai lay down on top of him tucking his head into the crook of Dane's neck.

After a long moment, Kai whispered, "Can you breathe now?"

"Barely."

Kai rolled them onto their sides and pulled the comforter up and over them both. His arms wrapped around Dane. Dane had never been this familiar in bed with a man he'd just met. His first times with his other male lovers had been cooler, more about the lust, less about the feeling, and they'd slept in the same bed but with distance between them.

Nothing matched this wildfire now. This was brand new.

They clutched each other for a long time. Dane felt his hand fall asleep again. He didn't care. He didn't want to move.

He sank into sleep as Kai's warm breath puffed steadily against his shoulder and neck.

Chapter Ten

Dane woke, blinking rapidly, realizing he must have completely passed out.

Too much wine? Too much sex?

Never with Kai.

The morning light filtered through the gray and black curtains, alighting on dust motes, turning the air the color of cider.

Kai slept tightly curled against Dane's side, one fisted hand under his chin. Yellow and copper bangs fell against his eyelids. The eyelashes were dark brown, creating a feathery line above his cheeks. His jaw and chin were rough with glints of gold new-morning beard. He was beautiful.

Dane reached out and brushed his hand across Kai's forehead, pressing his fingertips lightly to his soft hair.

Kai shifted with a soft sigh and slowly opened his eyes. His look was gentle and languid. He blinked once, then raised himself up on his elbow, pushing his hair back with his other hand.

"You're still here." Kai's voice broke the peace with his low monotone.

The hammering in Dane's chest quickened. His face warmed. Had he over-stepped his boundaries? He thought back quickly over the night's antics. Kai had never really invited him to stay the night. But the only time Kai had asked Dane to leave was after dinner. And then in the middle of the night, Kai had been afraid Dane had left.

"I—" Dane began.

"It's all right. But I need to get to work." The sheet fell from Kai's smooth chest, revealing lean muscles and pink nipples that perked up when the air hit them.

Kai glanced at Dane as though looking through him, not meeting his eyes, then turned and slid from the confines of the bed.

Blood rushed all through Dane's body to see him, angular, sculpted, lovely to behold. Kai moved naked across the room in the coppery morning light with confidence and grace, but also a quickness that belied some lingering shyness. Still, he was nothing like that awkward teen Dane remembered, stumbling to gather his papers, stricken at being bullied, hiding behind a hank of unkempt tangles. This man had grown tall in more ways than physical, and had taken his power back. But there was still a jerkiness there, a hint of vulnerability Kai didn't want to show. Was that why he was alone? Why he lived in such a huge house on a hill with no one but a butler?

A butler… In this day and age, who had one of those? The very rich had daily housekeepers, even cooks, but butlers?

Kai would not look at Dane now as he moved to the bathroom a little too fast, a little too eager to be away.

As Kai was disappearing into the bathroom, Dane's gaze lingered on the slim hips and perfect bend of ass. Dane's hands had touched him there. That softness. That lovely dip where thigh met curve. His fingers had delved carefully into the crease further inward, trailing along the secret heat there, silently wishing—*Some day, maybe. Some day.*

The door closed with a rather unpleasant thump, and Dane was left alone in the silence of the early morning shadows. At first he wasn't sure what to do. He moved his legs up in the bed, then sat up.

But of course he knew the next course of action. Of *polite* action. He needed to get up and gather his clothes and all his other bits. He needed to present himself to the day as a man unfazed, be a grown up and not presume upon another's intentions or generosity.

He must show Kai, through grace and dignity, that the date was a success, but not be too pushy as he had been last night when he hadn't left. And yet, if he had left, the wonderful past night would never have happened.

It had been wonderful. It had become far more than a charity "hook up" and his body quaked in a kind of panic to think that, because though Kai had been eager, maybe this session was just something Kai needed to get out of his system. Maybe Kai, who had his own huge life now, and could do anything at all, would move on.

Dane shook his head, eyes closing for a moment. Refusing the scenario.

But manners still had him immediately up and collecting his clothing, shoving his legs into his trousers, fastening the belt, locating his socks.

By the time Kai came out of the bathroom, Dane was standing shirtless by the big window where he'd parted the curtains. He'd been gazing out at the dew-glittered hills of the green back yard. Beyond the property, oaks shed earthen leaves under the glowing pink sky.

When he heard the bathroom door click open, Dane turned to look at Kai. Kai's hair was slicked back, a darker honey brown when wet and fresh from a shower. He wore dark blue trousers and a white shirt, half-buttoned, but his feet were still bare.

Dane smiled to see the man he'd spent the night with looking so polished and ready for the day. Kai made his heart trip up again, and it was a great feeling.

Kai met his eyes for only a second, then he moved to his dresser. "I know you have to get back to your car now. Do you want a shower first?"

"I need to shower before my shoot at noon. I'll do it at home."

"You have a shoot today?" Kai got out a pair of black socks and bent to put them on while standing.

"Yes. In L.A."

"I see. All right then."

Dane heard the crispness in the voice, the same way Kai had been when he'd thrown Dane out last night.

"Thank you for a great—um—date."

Now Kai turned, hopping a little as he got the second sock on his foot. "You're thanking me?"

Taken aback, Dane said, "For the dinner, the evening, um, well," he cleared his throat, thinking of their first kiss, the whisper of their lips, and how just that had been such a turn on, and of how they'd finally come together like two hot flames in the bed that was not more than eight feet away from them both right now. "Um--well— just thank you for everything."

"You don't have to thank me. I bought you. Remember?" Quite suddenly, Kai's voice had gone cold.

"Yes. I remember." Dane's own voice lowered and he felt it get lost in the back of his throat on the word *remember*.

Quite suddenly, Kai was sliding his feet into his shoes and snapping a Rolex to his wrist. He lifted his chin and threw his shoulders back as if compensating for a stiff muscle, or maybe he just didn't want to look anywhere but face-front.

"All right," Kai said, heading for the door. "I've gotta go. If you need anything, just ask Ben on your way out. I'll have the limo waiting for you."

Dane opened his mouth to speak but before he could answer, Kai was through the door and he heard him skipping down the stairs almost as if he were running.

Reeling, Dane looked about the silent, empty room. At first he could only take short, shallow breaths. Then he took another deeper breath. When he finally realized what had just happened, that he'd been summarily dismissed, he slumped.

"Fuck," he said to the rumpled bed. "Fuck."

Chapter Eleven

Before he left, Dane used the bathroom to wash up. It was a glorious marble creation, with gold, swan-necked faucets, and a room for the sinks alone so big he could have set up home there. The toilet had a separate room all to itself. It smelled of tulips with a background freshness that was never cloying, just pleasant.

He studied Kai's things on the counter. Not much. A toothbrush in a purple ceramic holder. A sleek shaving kit. A large, black brush with soft, white bristles. The place looked barely lived in. Either Kai was a minimalist, or he'd just moved in and hadn't had time to put any of his personality into his rooms.

It has hard to marvel at any of it, though. Dane's thoughts spun as he realized he might never see Kai again, or be invited back to this glorious abode.

He hurried to finish dressing and left as quickly as Kai had, taking the stair steps two at a time, coming into the shining front room where the high ceiling glimmered with a crystal chandelier.

Ben met him at the front door with a cup of coffee.

"I don't need it," Dane said, though the smell made him want to weep.

"Kai insisted. You may keep the mug."

Dane looked at the outstretched hand. The white mug was large with a wide bottom and curved at the top. It had a handle like the tapered body of a lady, but no, he was mistaken. That was a dragonfly body and the wings arched up to connect to the mug, helping to form the handle.

As Dane took the mug, a thought teased from deep within. *I'll keep it forever.*

He had to leave. He didn't want to leave.

The limo was purring at the edge of the drive. Sleek. Long-bodied. Darkened windows. The exhaust sent small white clouds on the morning air.

Dane blinked against the brightening sky. The horizon had lost its rosy tint. The night had really and finally ended.

The coffee steamed in his hand. Smelled slightly burnt, bitter and sweet.

The driver was the same young man from last night, impeccably dressed in a tuxedo. Kai had called him Mark.

"Good morning, sir." He opened the door and Dane slid wordlessly into the car and onto a slippery leather seat.

On the drive back to the community theatre, Dane saw images of trees, houses and fields pass by the windows, but never looked directly at them. He kept his gaze on his hands which were wrapped tightly about the warm mug. He focused on breathing.

It was as if he was being born into the world anew, but he didn't want that world. He wanted the one he was leaving behind. With all his heart. But slowly it was growing further and further away.

He couldn't hope that Kai might call him back. Today. Tomorrow. In a week. He couldn't think about the future. Futures looked grim and disappointing to young men who made their livings off youth and good looks that faded (according the industry standards) by age 30. Futures were for people who had love in their lives. Dane had never had that. He lived in the moment.

Now, in this moment, the limo pulled up behind his parked Infiniti in an asphalt parking lot in a little town he had once called home.

Dane held the coffee mug tightly in his hands. The coffee was cold now, the mug warmed only by the heat of his palms. When he got out of the limo, he almost dropped it. The driver held the door and caught his hand. The mug was saved.

He barely remembered the drive home.

In his condo kitchen, he set the pretty mug with the dragonfly handle on the countertop and went straight to the shower. The water fell over him, the warm streams perking him up a bit.

The rest of the morning went by quickly as he returned phone calls, talked to his agent about the big fashion industry party that night, and feasted on a handful of grapes. Sometimes he fasted before a shoot. But the grapes were irresistible.

By the time he walked onto the set of the noon photo shoot, he was perfectly groomed, rested, ready.

Or so he thought.

It was a part indoor, part outdoor shoot. Everything distracted him. Surprised him. The utter blue of the sky on a warm autumn day. The way the make up artist kept touching up the corner of his left eye. It stung as if he'd been burned. When the set director prodded his limbs, getting him in place, and the camera man kept asking him to move right, left, forward, he became confused and tried to hide it.

"Are you drunk?" came a soft voice from his right. Fitch, the director.

"No."

"All right, then. Pay attention. You're too beautiful and we don't want to waste any time getting as many shots as we can."

This time it was not an underwear ad. Though he didn't mind those, he was rather grateful, for he felt hot and half aroused and he couldn't seem to get complete control of himself.

This was an ad for spring. Always, the marketing was two seasons ahead.

Dane wore white linen shirts and soft jeans. Spring demanded a cool, fresh, composed look. He posed with flowers and a plaid umbrella. He posed in garden chairs and at patio tables with glasses of lemonade at hand. They had a machine that made fake mist and rain drops. He posed wet, which was good because he'd been sweating far too much after the first half hour. He posed in front of fans for a wind-blown look. They changed his outfits twenty-five times. The wardrobe guy was polite enough not to comment on how hot his skin was, and the perspiration there. Between each change of clothes, he wiped Dane down and re-dressed him in cool, dry garments.

By the time Dane finished the shoot, he was exhausted. Nervous. Still so hot.

He checked his phone over and over. He had received no calls. Not important ones, anyway. Nothing from Kai. Nothing.

Then he wondered. Did Kai even have his number? But of course he had to have it. From the auction paperwork. Surely Kai knew how to contact him.

Dane did not feel right about making the first move himself. He'd been Kai's guest. If he was to be invited back to the big house on the hill, Kai would have to make the move.

Fitch-the-director, whom he'd worked with before, clasped his hand about Dane's arm as Dane was leaving. Fitch was forty-one, had fake bleached hair, and wore black-framed glasses that made him look like an overly fashionable physicist.

"Are you okay?"

"Sure."

"You said not two words the whole afternoon."

"I'm fine."

"Well, whatever's bugging you, babe, the shoot went well. That dreamy look in your eyes was perfect. Tantalizing. So, you're coming to the party tonight, right? Everyone who's anyone is making an appearance."

Dane shook his head. He knew what it would consist of. Lots of booze and drugs. Pretty girls and boys schmoozing the producers, the designers, the wealthy patrons. A pool filled with fake blow-up swans sporting unopened champagne bottles and people talking fashion, fashion,

fashion, with their affected cackles and their lecherous gazes. And there would be paparazzi. And caviar. And those who were super impressed with themselves.

He'd been to dozens of these parties of the rich, the bold, the privileged, the beautiful. He'd been flattered at first to be included. Impressed for a while. But bored after a year. His career mattered to him a lot, so he played the game. But he never stayed for the after hours antics of drinking, for the expensive drugs, or for the sex. He didn't like to play so light and fast with his body and heart.

But now... He'd never felt this way before.

"You have to come," Fitch said. "Everyone loves you."

Dane smiled. "They do not."

"They do. You're the star focus right now. Your underwear ad is everywhere. People want to meet you. Know you. They love that you're gay, those who know. Those who don't... they love a mystery. You stay aloof. It's mesmerizing. When you're hot, you need to get out and make the most of it. Nothing lasts in this biz."

"I'm aware of that."

"So you're coming? Lots of celebs will be there. And your agent. You'll be part of that "in" crowd."

"Thanks. Maybe."

Fitch gave him directions to the place in the Hollywood Hills but Dane barely heard him. He couldn't think of champagne and roses and fame and fawning attention.

Accolades and connections. Limelight and success. None of that seemed to matter right now.

Right now, all he could think of was Kai.

He checked his phone again. Nothing.

Fitch patted him on the back. "You know what? I am going to make sure you come. I'm going to send a car for you."

Dane nodded and gave him his sheepish smile, the one that made everyone—except Kai, perhaps—want to hire him, fuck him, or place him as the central focus in their ads.

Fitch looked at him over the rim of his glasses and said, "It's settled then. See you there!"

*

On the way home to his condo, Dane watched the eastern sky turn lavender, then pink through his windshield. The bronzing sun in his rearview mirror set over the smoggy L.A. skyline giving everything a sepia tint.

When Dane reached his exit off the freeway, he had a thought to pass it by, to keep driving until he reached the foothills of L.A. County and the road to Kai's house. He didn't know the exact route to get there, but he was sure he could find it by trial and error.

But his hands turned the steering wheel, and he took his own exit as he always did, swift and smooth, going a little over the speed limit because he knew the way blind. He'd owned his condo for a year now, bought with the proceeds from his career. When he was in New York, he was comped free temporary condos and hotel rooms by the industry. But in L.A. he had wanted to have his own place.

Five minutes later he was parked and unlocking the door to his home.

The first thing he saw as he walked through his living room was the kitchen counter and the white dragonfly handle mug that sat there still half-filled with dark liquid.

For long seconds he stood staring at it. Ben the butler had given it to him. But he'd said it had been a gift from Kai.

He'd forgotten.

Dane's mind wanted to make meaning out of it. Was this was Kai's calling card? Kai's way of placing his mark, his promise?

But promise of what?

Connection?

Dane's skin heated at the thought. Perspiration broke out on his back. An inner tremble tightened his muscles.

Then why doesn't he call me?

He turned away, leaving the mug where it stood, and headed for the bedroom.

The limo was coming round at eight. He only had time for a quick shower and a protein bar. He didn't like snacking too much at the parties. He needed to keep himself lean and hungry-looking.

He'd eaten very little today. Some grapes. And some yogurt from the buffet at the shoot. But right now he felt overly hungry. Too hungry for everything, as if a new version of Dane was trying to claw its way out of his pre-Kai existence. His body seemed raw and sensitive.

In the shower, his second of the day, when he touched the inner skin of his thighs his fingertips burned. He soaped up quickly. Rinsed. Shampooed.

These events—the after-hour parties—were for and about fashion even if people insisted the parties were for relaxation. The one tonight was a whopper. Terry, Dane's agent, had been talking about it for weeks.

Dressing in a designer black suit, dark purple shirt and no tie was just barely appropriate. He slipped into his Ferragamos, which seemed to impress everyone but him. They were so soft inside he did not need socks. He liked that part.

Unlike Kai, he did not have a Rolex, but he did have a silver bracelet cuff he liked and a silver ring band for his middle finger.

He let his dark hair dry loose, tapered back about his shoulders, bangs in his eyes which he knew he would keep pushing back from his face all night. It was probably the wrong move not to gel it, but he preferred it that way, casual and free.

Several times as he was dressing he caught himself losing focus, standing still and staring at nothing. Several times he almost picked up his phone and cancelled the limo.

He was not in the mood for a party. He wanted to stay home and sit. Sit and wait. Wait for Kai to call.

His stomach growled. He thought to stay home, fix a lite microwave frozen dinner. But when the limo showed up he went to meet it, got in, and let it whisk him to the Hollywood Hills.

He couldn't help but think, as he watched the flashing of the lights from the freeway and surrounding cities they passed, they were headed in the wrong direction. He wanted to go east. Further into the hills that bordered the mountains and deserts of southern California.

He wanted to go up a familiar, winding autumn road and stop at the gate framed by darkly blushing bougainvillea blossoms, watch it open for him as they glided toward the flagstone front drive. He wanted to see that shining front door, the stained glass dragonflies, and more, the man inside with the tight posture and tilted head welcoming him. Or frowning at him. Either way, he wanted to see him.

Dane looked at his phone again and again. He had a text from his agent. *Will u b there 2nite?* He had another from Fitch. *C U soon.* And others from various people he worked with.

It was all about nothing. Nothing that mattered to him, anyway.

Chapter Twelve

Someone brushed by him a little too drunken and rough.

"Pretty boy," the man whispered, then cackled.

Dane looked for Fitch, or his agent. Or Taffy who did the make up on half his shoots, who he liked very much. Or anyone else he might know. But the crowd came on thick and redolent with Maison Francis, Armani and Clive Christian colognes. Through flashing bulbs and laughter and expensively made up stares, Dane made his way, stopped half a dozen times by strangers who wanted to shake his hand, or by photographers getting in his face, snapping photos, many asking inappropriate private and personal questions.

Sometimes he remembered to smile.

Again, he wondered why he'd bothered to come. This was about people wanting to be "in," to be seen. That need to feel important and wonderful was addictive. Dane had the urge, to be sure, but after last night with Kai, everything looked like paste-glitter, cheap and flimsy and fake.

He saw clearly now through his tired eyes. The scuff marks on the suede thigh-high boots worn by sixteen year old girl models. The flesh so stretched and botoxed on the older ones, both male and female, it hardly moved, the hair sprayed until it was like rock. He saw distracted, empty faces high on alcohol and more, ready for any pleasure they could get, euphoric, high-strung, happy all the while until they went home to their echoing houses and faced themselves alone. Scared it would all go away. Feeling unloved if they weren't perfect perfect perfect.

That was how Dane had felt off and on for his whole career. Last night, Kai had been the one to punch his bubble. He hadn't realized it until the photo shoot when all he could see was the fake and fleeting luster of the set and the role he played and the director accusing him of being drunk. All that mattered was he wanted to reach out to Kai again.

Please call.

When Dane finally found his agent, Terry, the man took him aside with a strange, bewildered smile. That always meant bad news.

"New York Threads is going with Bjin for their spring spread. It's all okay, though. You're solidly booked, and I'll see to it that something else fills that slot for you. The potential loss is 50k but you won't feel it. You're still on the shortlist for the Anais commercial. By the end of this year you'll be in the seven figure range after all those billboard royalties. Maybe more."

"It's okay." But it really wasn't. Bjin with his funny single name was up and coming. A contender. The competition.

"He's only sixteen," Terry said. His breath smelled of Scotch. "He knows nothing of the biz. They'll be exasperated with him after five minutes. He won't be able to hold a pose or contend with the elements. Especially since his mommy always tags along."

Dane nodded as if he cared. A part of him did care. For the past four years he'd lived in a world of ice people. Loyalty was an unknown word. Scandals, whether they were true or not, caused sponsors to quickly change their tunes. You were in one day. Out the next.

"Don't let it get to you."

"I'm not," Dane said quietly.

Terry took a drink from a passing waiter, a skinny flute of champagne, and handed it to Dane. "You're on your way to super stardom. You have the looks and the composure. The talent."

"I'm not worried." Dane lied. He was worried. Always had been. He turned twenty-five in a few months. Next year his career could be over.

124

"Fitch said you were preoccupied today. Everything okay?"

Dane nodded, pretending to sip the champagne.

"Good. How'd that charity thing you said you were doing go? It was such small potatoes I figured it'd waste your time. Did you land a good date?"

"Yep. It was fine. My hometown. Small deal but they appreciated that I showed up."

"Good for you, kid."

After their little chat, Terry took him by the arm and introduced him to a dozen people, praising his glory and traits. Selling him.

It seemed everywhere he went, people were buying him.

Even last night. With Kai.

At the thought, a pang of disappointment stabbed him deep in the chest. Kai had bought him. Rejected him. Then taken him back. Taken him to bed. That was all. Not such a big deal.

Sweat broke out all over his body. He had never felt so lost before, so strangely excited and sad at the same time. He wanted to laugh loudly and drink all night. He wanted to retreat to a corner and huddle into himself. He wanted to dive into the pool stay down at the bottom in silence forever. His mind was a whirl.

He shook hands and smiled, knowing his dimples showed and his dark eyes glimmered in the soft party lights. He kept pushing his hair back from his forehead. When he did that, people grinned at him, looking underfed, overzealous, turned on.

But when he saw the kid by the pool, relaxing in a lime green lounge chair surrounded by people laughing and talking, his stomach flipped.

Bjin.

"You didn't tell me he was here," Dane said to Terry.

"Oh, yeah."

The new princeling with the single name. All the rage.

They'd never met, but Dane was all-too aware of him. Terry made sure of that. Had talked about landing Bjin's contract for himself—to represent the enemy?—but missed the opportunity by a thread. Terry never let Dane forget the kid was beginning to win jobs with many of Dane's more solid corporations.

Bjin had a leanness and sadness that could not be faked. His eyebrows arched high, but his eyes swooped in a downward grace that made them look perfectly painted onto his face in a compellingly heartbroken, sorrow-mask. He had Dane's coloring although Bjin's eyes were brown, not blue. And no dimples, but a more youthful, virginal bearing. It was irksome at best.

Dane had become so used to attention that he had not realized how many people had been surreptitiously following him and Terry about the party. Photographers. Admirers. Spies. Wanna-bees who were guests of directors and producers. Or people who simply liked to stare at celebs.

But now he noticed when they all converged away from him and toward Bjin who sat up and smiled in a doleful but happy way, showing his perfectly capped white teeth. Not even a pimple marred the boy's perfection.

Dane turned to Terry. "I'm not feeling well. I think I'll leave early."

"You can't leave! You have to meet him."

"I don't."

"You must. For appearance's sake." Terry clasped his arm again, tighter now, and led him forward.

Dane smiled. And smiled some more when everyone wanted them to pose together for various Internet and Youtube channels. Or freebies for blogs and websites that published junk about parties like these.

Bjin's hand was cold when Dane politely shook it. For a mere sixteen year old, he was already as tall as Dane. His look was endearingly melancholy when he said his formal "hello" but a shark rested deep in those dark eyes that met Dane's. Terry had lied when he'd said the kid didn't know anything about the biz.

Suddenly, Dane was hating every moment of this party. Of his job. His life.

He kept remembering the night before, Kai glancing away from him, chin held high, then finally letting him into his bedroom, his bed, his arms.

Kai played the same roles as so many of the people at this party. Donning the façade of success and power to hide the hurt, the loneliness of real life. Everyone did it. They had their comforts to deal with life, whether it was alcohol, or a job, or hobby. But still, Kai was far more real to Dane after just one night than any of these party-goers.

The only way Dane could get away from attention at these parties was when he needed to use the john. Now he made his polite and graceful excuse.

He felt Terry's lingering look on the back of his neck. His agent loved to control his clients even to the timing of when they pissed.

Well, he wasn't going to piss.

He headed toward the downstairs restroom just for show. There was a line anyway. There always was. Just as well he didn't need the facilities.

He turned past that short hallway and out onto a side patio that led to a view of dark lawns leading toward a far lane swept by indistinct and shadowy trees. A cool breeze ruffled Dane's loose hair.

Dim lights cast odd brown shadows across this secluded patio. A potted juniper against one wall afforded him the cover he needed. He stood to the side of it furthest from the sliding glass door.

He leaned against the wall, breathing the dusty, sharp scent of the tree and stared at his lit phone.

He knew nothing about Kai except his first name and the name of his company. He did not have his number but he might be able to find it. So that was where he started.

With his smart phone it was easy to get the information for Kai's company. He called there first. It was after hours so all he could do was leave a message on Kai's answering service. It gave him Kai's full name. Kyle Northwood. It was the first time he'd heard the man's last name. Dane left his own full name and the time. Then he added:

If you get this, call me back when you find the time.

He added his phone number. But he was sure Kai had it.

It was a lame message. Pathetic sounding.

He bit his lower lip hard in self-punishment.

Next, he found Kai's email. He pondered for a long time over the blank space and finally bailed off the screen. He could not find the right words to write him a message. Anything he thought of sounded stupid.

Desperate, he found the email page again. Stared at it. Then entered his name and phone number and email. That was all. Before he chickened out again he hit *send*.

He felt like an idiot.

Searching for Kai on Facebook, he found nothing. He looked on Instagram. Still nothing. Even Googling his name came up with only bare, simple profiles, or brief articles mentioning him in business blogs or magazines. Connecting with Kai in any casual manner, other than business, apparently was impossible.

Lowering himself to the patio floor on his knees and sitting back on his heels, Dane leaned against the wall and stared into the darkness. The rolling lawns gave off scents of newness mixed with the smoky autumn promise of winter round the bend. He loved it, but it also filled him with an odd despair. This was the second giant house on a hill he'd been to in two nights. He should have seen it as the circle widening, his travels coming to a head, all his dreams and drive to succeed made manifest.

Instead, he saw the circle tightening.

There was Bjin. Of course that hurt, but not really. He expected Bjins in this business. They came out of the very structure, parting the fabrics of the runway curtains with their elegant hands and proclaiming themselves to the world.

Bjins were everywhere. Dane still had the now famous underwear ad on billboards, cab-cars, buses, subways, and magazines. He had too many contracts to count and Terry was still on his side. For a while. Until Terry landed his own Bjin and forgot Dane.

But he was okay for now. He was fine. Everyone still wanted a piece of him.

He was seen.

That was the crux of it, wasn't it?

He heard Kai's voice. *You didn't see me.*

Yes, that was the core of every human's life. The need to be seen, heard. Validated. Dumb as that was, human beings were such a lonely lot.

Dane gritted his teeth at the thought. He ran his hand through his hair for the hundredth time. In his other hand, he held tightly to his phone as if it were a creature with a heartbeat all its own. As if it might disappear if he let go for a second and looked the other way.

Stupid.

He took deep breaths of the fresh air. The dew of nighttime temporarily dissipated the L.A. smog. It was the best time to be out in the heart of Hollywood.

Kai's voice came back to him again. *I followed you around. Learned about you. You didn't even notice.*

High school. What a weird place full of lost and lonely young humans. Kai had followed him. Kai knew things about him. Kai had been stalking him?

He let out a quiet laugh. Stalking. Such a bad word. But he was flattered to hear it now. And chagrined at himself for never noticing. Well, he'd certainly noticed Kai now. His lips curved up at the thought.

As if on cue, Dane's phone gonged. Amid all the earlier texts from the day, this one stood out. A single question mark.

It was from Kai.

His heart rate went up. Kai had answered. Dane had somehow gotten through!

But how did one answer a single question mark? What did that even mean? Was Kai saying that Dane was intruding and he sent the mark to denote annoyance? Or was he asking for Dane to answer him with a clear intent? For admittedly, Dane's messages themselves had been cold.

Not knowing what to do—again—Dane's fingers hovered over the digital keyboard.

Finally, he hit the question mark symbol, then *send*.

He chastised himself for having no words of his own, for copying what the other man had done. He'd been the one to contact Kai. He needed to come clean.

His phone emitted a gong.

Kai had answered.

Are you upset or something?

Trying to curb his growing excitement, Dane replied, *What? No. I was just bored.*

He regretted that one, too, as soon as he sent it.

What are you doing?

Sitting in the dark.

That new up and comer is an upset to the industry, isn't he? Bjin?

How do you know?

I am a business man. I know business.

Not fashion.

Why do you think I don't keep up on fashion?

Indeed, how did Dane know? The boy Kai had been had followed him around high school and Dane had never known.

Dane typed, *Do you keep up?*

130

I'm gay and I have money to burn. What do you think?

Dane pressed down on his smile. *I think that's a cliché. Who's a cliché Mr. Underwear God?*

Dane chuckled. They were texting. There was humor. That was huge.

He heard the slide of a glass door on rails nearby. Looked up.

Kai was immaculate in his Armani suit, dark golden hair spiked a little at the forehead, the dimness making his eyes black as space.

Came the soft voice, "What in the hell are you doing in the shadows of this glitz and glam gala event?"

Dane could no longer suppress his smile. "Oh my god, what are you doing here?"

Everything in his body soared upward to see Kai standing in front of him. He pushed himself from the wall and rose to full height.

"If I said I stalked you, would you call the police?"

"Nooo." Dane was laughing. He moved forward thinking to clasp Kai on the arm when suddenly the entire patio lit up with cameras and the party-goers who followed them.

"There's Dane!" someone said.

Kai stepped back just as Dane raised his hand.

A crowd of people in diamonds and black lace loomed in between them, followed by a cloud of alcohol and perfume and the cloying scent of hairspray mixed with sweat. In a patter of confusion, Dane was pelted with questions.

"What do you think of Bjin taking your contract with Threads?"

"Do you and Bjin know each other?"

"Do you see Bjin as a competitor?"

"Do you see age as a barrier for you in the near future?"

"What's your next deal?"

"Are you going to fast-track to New York or take it easier in L.A.?"

And many, many more he could not make sense of.

Dane knew the game. He had to smile. He had to give them his business face, the pretty boy who right now graced the world wearing nothing but tan, lean muscles and tight briefs.

"Bjin is beautiful," he heard himself saying. "In this business I think there is room for us both. He has a completely different look and style."

But as he was speaking, he kept rising on his tiptoes, trying to see over the shoulders of the crowd, looking for Kai who had completely disappeared from view.

He flashed his dimples with a half open-mouthed smile. And kept glancing around for Kai.

"Excuse me." Dane tried to push his way through the milling people. There were so many. Well, he was the popular guy of the moment.

While being photographed and questioned, it was a rude gesture to check his phone. But he did it anyway.

As if Kai would text him while he was being interviewed. Not a chance.

But would Kai stick around for it?

Slim chance there, too. Kai had already been pushed around and ignored in his early years. And Dane had been a part of that, even if by proxy. But he was a big man in his own right now. He wouldn't stand for it.

Desperate, he shoved one man aside who grumbled an offended, "Hey!" Dane shimmied his way toward the edge of the patio where Kai had been standing. No sign of him.

"Kai!" Dane called out.

People started calling Dane's name again, drowning him out.

"*Kai!*"

Dane looked toward the lawn for human shadows outside the patio structure and saw nothing but the rolling expanse of dark green and dusky tree shadows beyond. He turned toward the sliding glass door and saw only the open byway leading back to the soft lights of the party and the drunken, busy voices within the rooms and out on the bigger patio by the pool.

He didn't see Kai, but Kai still might have gone back inside.

"Kai!" he called again. No answer.

He pushed past the crowd, which didn't seem to want to let him go.

"Damn it," he said.

Someone probably got that cuss word on audio. He didn't care. Once inside, he moved quickly through the house all the way to the front door. No Kai.

He headed for the pool. Bjin still sat entertaining another large crowd.

Dane stepped behind a curtain and scanned the area. Nothing.

He went back to the smaller, side patio. A lot of the party-goers and photographers had scattered and the glass, sliding door remained open. Some people had wandered to a wrought-iron table there, and sat in some chairs.

Dane jogged past them to the edge of the bricks where they met the lawn. He breathed the night air deeply into his lungs, trying to quell his disappointment.

Kai had come all this way only to abandon him? It didn't make sense.

Stepping onto the slightly damp lawn, Dane had the thought that he could walk the grounds, all the way around the property, including the front where the limos dropped people off and picked them up on the long, wide circular drive. Maybe Kai was there waiting to leave….

The grass was a thick cushion under his feet.

He headed away from the party, and though he was tense about Kai leaving, already he felt himself relax. Here he was, somewhat famous, and he hated crowds.

As he moved into the anonymity of the shadows and the lure of the trees toward the property's edge, he thought he saw a flash of light. Probably someone had come outside for a smoke, but he decided to check it out anyway.

As Dane came closer to the light, he saw glints of blond-brown hair, bright even in the tree shadows, and the silhouetted line of the cleanly cut Armani suit.

Of course Kai had come out here. He had led Dane the night before to a peaceful, secret place on his own estate where he said he liked to hang out and look at the stars. Kai liked trees. Solitude. Peace.

Dane glanced at the burning glow in Kai's right hand.

"Are you smoking?"

"I'm not smoking. I'm checking my phone." Kai's voice was nonchalant.

"Oh." Dane could see now that the red light he thought was the hot end of a cigarette was actually Kai's phone half-obscured by his hand.

Dane put his own phone into his jacket pocket.

Kai stood with his shoulders slightly hunched, head tilted down as he gazed at his phone. His body language conveyed a closed attitude, but maybe that was because of the phone.

All Dane wanted to do was touch him. His body reacted to the man's presence immediately.

Back on the patio, when Kai had first spoken, the shakiness within him which he'd felt all day increased. Now his mind fixated on visions and feelings from their night together. How Kai had felt in his arms both clothed and unclothed. Slippery. Lean. Hot. And how eager Dane felt when they made love, yearning not to have that moment end, hoping the night could last forever.

"I wanted to know," Dane began. His throat went immediately dry. He croaked out the rest of his question. "How did you know about this party?"

"I told you."

"You were joking when you said you were stalking me."

"I was?" Kai did not look up from his phone.

"Um, I don't--" Dane couldn't finish.

"I'm an expert with computers, apps, gps, all that."

"Right," Dane said. "So you found me."

Kai shrugged, still not looking up.

Dane really liked it that Kai had been looking for him. And found him.

"I didn't want to come to this party," Dane said.

"Why not? Isn't it part of the job? You need to be seen."

There were those words again. *To be seen.* It was about that when they were young. And now as well. Dane had been seen. Kai had been invisible. And even though he was probably one of the wealthier attendees at this event, Kai was still invisible.

But this wasn't Kai's playground, Dane told himself. At Kai's place of work, Dane would be the invisible one.

Or maybe, just maybe, all this was never about being seen to the world at large. It was about Kai not being seen by Dane when they were teens. And now?

Dane took a tentative step forward. "I want to leave."

Now Kai looked up. "What?"

"I want to go."

"All right."

Dane gave a short sigh. "Come with me."

"I think maybe you should come with me. I brought my own limo."

"Yeah?"

"Yeah."

The blood in Dane's veins quickened. His body anticipated holding Kai faster than his brain could comprehend how lovely it would be. It was hot, now, in the autumn shadows. A slight stinging sensation ran up and down his back, arms and legs.

Dane did not hesitate to move toward the front of the house on the other side of the rolling lawn. The lights gleamed in the distance. The house itself blocked most of the drive, but pulsed bright arcs upon the air.

Dane nearly stumbled in his haste. As he caught himself, he looked over his shoulder. Kai still stood under the trees, fiddling with his phone.

Taking a deep breath, Dane looked up, trying to see the stars through the haze of L.A. Only a few prickled the night with their distant heat. Everything about them seemed so lonely.

"Kai?" he asked.

Kai looked up. "Hmm, coming."

Dane felt his face break into a lopsided smile.

"What?" Kai asked as he came alongside him. "In a hurry or something?"

Something. But Dane did not answer out loud.

Chapter Thirteen

This was a different limo. With creamy bucket seats that faced each other back to front, a moon roof, and a full bar.

And here he was, Dane the super-model, gliding off to a beautiful rendezvous with a guy he could not stop thinking about. He'd had a full day. He'd hardly eaten. He should have been exhausted. All his hunger, and all his energy ramped up. The only feast he wanted was Kai. To touch. To hold. To kiss. He wanted to do that all night if Kai would let him. Dane's energy thrummed, limitless.

They were facing each other. Kai was looking away from him and out the window, phone still in hand. His other hand lay curled against his thigh. Dane reached out and put his hand on the top of Kai's wrist.

Kai turned to look at him, green eyes deep, the pupils huge and dark.

"Don't." Kai pulled his hand back.

"What?"

Kai's lips flattened to neither a scowl nor a smile. Dane had yet to see a real smile from him.

"Not yet," Kai said.

Dane sat back. Rejected. Heart open and aching. Kai had to know that Dane wanted him. Again. Or maybe he didn't? Maybe Kai wanted to be wooed. But how?

"Okay," Dane said slowly. He wanted to make light of it because the edge of his desire was cutting deep as if it battered naked against Kai's deflections. "Coffee first?"

At that, Kai smiled. "Have you eaten?"

Dane did not relish that much of a delay. So he lied. "Yes." Besides, the night was getting late.

"All right, then, I'll just have coffee sent up to our room."

"Our room?"

"I just booked one at the Brenton."

"What?"

"It's a four star. Is that not good enough?"

"We're going to a hotel?" Entirely flustered now, Dane shifted uncomfortably, his ass sliding against the bucket seat's sides.

"Yes. You thought something else?"

"Well, yes. I mean—"

Kai smiled now. Not the kind of smile Dane had been hoping for since they'd first met. And it wasn't exactly friendly. "You may have spent last night at my home, but normally that is not my process."

"Normally? Your process?" His mouth went dry again. He wanted water. Or better, whiskey, now that Kai was succeeding in quickly throwing him off. For this wasn't a game for Dane anymore. Without even thinking, he opened the fridge of the bar and found just what he wanted. He took the bottle and a glass from a holder.

Kai said, "That's not coffee."

In a clipped tone, Dane said, "I'm aware of that."

"Pour two," Kai ordered.

Dane glanced alongside his arm at him and then away again. He got out another glass.

The liquid poured brown as honey, promising a false warmth and the erasure of unwanted shock. What was Kai doing? What was he trying to say? That Dane was a "process"? Nobody more or less special than anyone else Kai might have met?

It was a blow. And his ego tanked. After he handed Kai his glass of whiskey, Dane up-ended his own and poured himself more.

He felt it go all the way down into his empty stomach, burning strokes of fire like an apocalypse of the heart. The limo hit a bump in the road. Whiskey splashed over the edges of his glass as he poured. As he tried to catch his breath.

138

He sat back in his seat, holding both the bottle and the glass.

Kai stared at him with cool intensity. "You don't want to go to a hotel?" he asked.

Dane wanted Kai. Badly. He desired him any way he could have him. But this? The insult was raw. He wanted to say no. But his body said any room, any bed would do. Because he was afraid if he said no that Kai would block him even more, and that would be that. The end of their "fling" or whatever was going on between them.

"So—" Dane sipped his second drink slowly this time. "You do this a lot?"

Kai raised an eyebrow at him. Took a drink.

"Well?" Dane prompted. His thoughts went back to the previous evening. How Kai had been sometimes endearingly tentative, sometimes clinging. How they'd held hands all the way up the staircase to Kai's suite. How Kai had slept tight against Dane's side. How they'd made love a second time in the middle of the night without words, and how good that had been. So good.

Kai had not brought him home to play with. They had not just fucked. They had made love. It had been reverent, sweet, even. Dane had not wanted to leave.

Now he had doubts that Kai had actually felt the same. How could he have read him so wrong? A hotel was a place of coldness, business. Hook ups.

Finally, Kai answered. "What I don't do is take strangers into my own bed."

Dane blinked rapidly. Strangers. That's what they really were to each other. Of course. And Dane's own feelings? They were feelings of flattery, perhaps, mixed with guilt for not seeing Kai in the earlier years when Kai was the victim of bullies and invisibility. That was all.

Then why were his eyes prickling?

Dane felt a deep quaking within. He wanted Kai. His body didn't care where they got together, whether they fucked or made love. But his heart—his mind—

"Can you stop the limo?"

"Of course," Kai said.

Dane took another large sip of his drink.

"You don't want to go to the Brenton?" Kai asked. And just like that, his voice had lowered, as if shy or unsure or quietly angered.

Dane shook his head no.

"Why not? It's beautiful."

"I'm sure it is," Dane said. He poured himself more whiskey. What had he been thinking? They barely knew each other. And all his swirling emotions—he was a fool!

He could only stare at the amber dregs in his glass. But he felt Kai studying him, a steady calm that was both annoying and fascinating.

"What if I said please?" Kai asked.

Dane looked up. Kai was still emotionless, sitting like a perfect, handsome man conducting a business meeting.

"Seriously?"

Kai nodded.

"Why?"

"I said why."

"You don't take strangers to your bed."

Kai nodded again.

Dane took a gulp of his drink this time, downing it all. Pouring more. "All right, then. Get me drunk enough, I'm yours."

"Why are you being this way?" Kai asked.

"Why are you?"

"Because—" Then Kai must have thought better of finishing and sat back in a slump.

Outside, the garish lights of the cities between Hollywood and Los Angeles flashed over them through the moon roof, hurting Dane's eyes. Alcohol made them sensitive.

140

But other parts of him became desensitized, and it was, right now, for the better.

The freeway was crowded for the late hour, but it was always like that here. Over-crowded, hard-edged, everyone looking to be somewhere they never really got to.

Dane studied Kai now, who was looking out the windows. By the end of his fourth drink, he had a realization. Maybe Kai needed a buffer. The idea of the hotel was that buffer. Maybe Kai needed to know he was protected. Safe. Because he cared.

At the sudden understanding, Dane relaxed a little. Kai cared. Maybe too much. And so did Dane. They were on the same page. Hopefully. It would just take a little time.

Okay, I can play this game, too.

"It's okay," Dane said, keeping his voice soft. "The hotel. I just don't usually do that."

"So do you simply go home with strangers and spend the night, then?"

"No. Not that, either."

Kai's chest expanded as he breathed in. "Well. Then."

"Yeah. Well." Dane nodded. "It's okay. I'm drunk enough now." He showed his dimples. It always got him acquiescence at the very least.

Now Kai scowled. "Good thing I'm having coffee ordered up to our room."

Dane suppressed a frown and poured himself another whiskey.

Kai held out his glass for more.

The city lights swooped over them like fluttering, luminous owls, strobing the limo's interior. Sitting still as prey caught in the night's lights, Kai looked more handsome than ever.

Dane's body heated once again. His mind ached for an end to this awkwardness, for all he wanted to do was love this man. He knew that now. His crime would be if he lost faith in himself. This night, he decided, must be handled delicately. It mattered a hell of a lot to him.

Finally, he put the whiskey away.

Chapter Fourteen

Dane had never been to the Brenton. Sporting spectacular fountains out front, tall palms for an "oasis" feel, and a circular drive with marble cut-outs shaped like seagulls, it loomed over the city of West L.A. in a posh neighborhood of fancy restaurants and designer clothing shops.

Kai's limo brought them to the front drop-off, then rolled away to gods-knew-where for the evening.

"Where does your driver go? Is he on call 24 hours?" Dane imagined him waiting around until he was called, living in the front seat, dedicated to his job.

Kai scrunched his lips together. "He has shifts just like any job. He's not my only driver."

"But where does he park while he's waiting?"

"I told him to go home and be back here by eight unless I call him. He actually lives nearby. Is that all right for you?"

Dane frowned. Nodded. He had nothing planned. But Kai could have asked.

He looked up at the bright façade of the hotel. The fountains clattered behind them, misting the air, smelling of spring.

Glitz. Glamour. The interior of the hotel sparkled.

They went in and Kai walked up to the curving check-in desk with nothing but his aura of charisma surrounding him. Dane stayed back by the couches in an area where the marble floor gave way to dark, maroon carpeting.

Well-dressed people milled about, and one well-behaved child. Dane could hear low voices and clinking sounds coming from a nearby bar. And further off, music. It was either a very big bar, or there were two bars down here in the lobby.

The awkwardness had not passed. To offset that, he grabbed his phone and looked for messages. He had some from his agent. *Did u leave early? Something I said?*

There were a few other unimportant ones. Acquaintances he barely knew who called him *friend*. He had few real friends and kept in touch with no one from high school.

The last text said, *Very nice to meet you.* It was from Bjin.

Just seeing that made words cross Dane's mind that were not fit to repeat. Words he never used. But why should he care about Bjin? More, he cared about who had shared his private number with the boy.

He looked up just as Kai approached, key in hand.

"You look like you just got a text that the world is about to explode."

"The world will go on forever. It's humans who are mortal," Dane said.

Kai glanced down at his plastic card key. "Well, we're set."

Dane felt his eyebrows tense. He looked at the key in Kai's hand and his stomach flipped. That text had not helped his mood. The whiskey sat in his stomach like sludge jostling about every time he moved.

Kai made a gesture for him to follow. He thought about standing very still, closing his eyes, wishing the text had actually been about the world going away. Why was he so bothered?

The hotel. Kai's casualness. Bjin. This was nothing he couldn't handle. But it was everything he did not want to handle.

Shoving his phone in his jacket pocket, he clenched his hands into fists and followed Kai to the elevators.

This wasn't what he wanted. Well, then, what did he want?

Kai in his arms. Yes. But in a place away from people. Kai's home. His own condo. Anywhere but here.

144

I don't invite strangers into my bed, Kai had said. Well what was last night, then? Plus, there was high school. Technically, they weren't strangers.

A drop of sweat dripped down the back of Dane's neck. Great. Now he was going to stink if he perspired all over his clothing.

Kai did not look at him as they entered the elevator. Dane watched the red digital numbers flash up and up and up. All the way to twenty-one, the topmost floor.

It figured. Kai had gotten them a suite.

Again, he wanted to back off. This was stupid. Why was Kai doing this? But he geared himself up for a good time. It would be wonderful to feel that smooth skin against his own again, hold that tense, ready-to-fly-away body in his arms. Like holding onto a shuddering, wild creature that wanted to flee but couldn't because you had the food and it was so, so hungry.

He could deal with anything if he got to feel Kai again, kiss him, breathe him. Everything else could languish on the back-burner. Kai would be his.

The elevator doors opened.

The hall was golden and white, the carpet a cream-colored thick spread that was so plush it almost felt like tripping to walk upon it. And yet it caught the soles of the feet just right, pushing up and back, as if to aid tired feet in getting you to your room.

Kai went to 2112 and keyed the door open.

Dane did not want to see inside at first. But then he couldn't hold back. The room was chrome and black and white, and the huge windows looked over the sprawling glitter of L.A. for miles and miles, all the way to a darkness that could be nothing other than the sea.

The bed was up on a low loft, three steps up, the area of that space fenced in by chrome bars polished to a mirrored shininess. Stacked with white and black pillows, the bed had a black over-spread at the foot, and a white comforter beneath, not too different from Kai's bed in Kai's own house.

There was a checkerboard floor at the entryway leading to a wave pattern that ended in black carpet. One wall was made up entirely of mirrors.

Dane stepped in. The door clicked shut at his back.

Kai tilted his head up. "Well?"

Dane nodded. "It's overwhelming."

"The best they had."

Dane forced a smile. "It's cold in here, though." One moment he'd been sweating and the next he had chills.

"I told you I'm having coffee brought up."

Dane let out a soft breath.

"And," Kai continued. "I'll turn up the heat."

Dane wanted to roll his eyes. He refrained from making a joke of what Kai had just said, but he'd set himself up so beautifully.

"It's all right. I don't like sleeping when the room is too warm." He deliberately said the word "sleeping" just to see if Kai would react.

Kai shrugged. Then moved forward to explore the room.

Dane found a black chair that looked comfortable and sat, leaning his head in his hands. He closed his eyes and a dizziness overtook him. He watched the swirling mist upon the blackness of his eyelids for awhile before opening them again.

A knock came at the door.

"Coffee's here," Kai said from across the room.

That was fast.

A man in a red uniform rolled a cart into the room. It was much more than coffee.

Dane blinked up from his chair watching as he set things up on a table for two by the window below the loft where the bed sat. Plates. Coffee cups. Champagne flutes. A bottle on ice. A covered food tray with steam wafting up, and

146

scents of seared meat, broccoli, and something sweet and hot like cobbler. Or pie.

Dane's stomach sloshed, then growled, then sloshed again. He tried not to groan.

After a few hushed words with Kai and a tip, the caterer left. Kai turned to Dane, hands out as if in question.

"It's a bit more than coffee," Dane protested.

"You don't have to eat. But I was hungry."

Dane got up and walked over to the table. Steaks. And broccoli. A tossed salad. And yes, that looked like fresh, hot peach cobbler on the side with a bowl of homemade whipped cream on ice.

Kai poured creamer into one of the coffee mugs. Then he handed it to Dane. "Here. Or do you like it sweeter?"

Dane did like sweet coffee. Sweet anything. But he refrained. It was the job.

He took the coffee. The mug was very white and the brown liquid within smooth and redolent. He tested a sip on his tongue. Not too hot to burn. Perfect. Not even bitter.

He held the cup out. "I think I will have one sugar."

Kai picked up a lump with tongs and tossed it in with a gentle splash.

Why had Kai done all this? He didn't want to take Dane home, yet he'd just now spent a fortune. On this night. On Dane.

"How did they get all this prepared so fast?" Dane asked.

"I texted ahead."

Dane sipped his coffee, watching as Kai sat and began to salt and pepper his steak. His body craved the coffee as he drank, and he realized he was gulping it now.

Kai took a big bite of rare meat. It was too much. His last good meal had been the dinner Kai had served him more than 24 hours ago.

Dane sat and after pouring himself another cup of coffee, neatly sliced his broccoli and began to eat. Veggies first. It was how he taught himself to eat so he wouldn't over-eat. Get full on salad and veggies, and you won't over-indulge on the rest. But he was very hungry tonight.

Kai looked like an angel in this light, his cheeks hollowing as he chewed, his lips glistening.

Dane took a bite of his steak and savored it. Now he did roll his eyes. But not in mocking dissent. This was pure pleasure.

"I think you don't eat enough."

Dane swallowed. "I watch the intake."

"Why? You don't have an ounce of fat on you."

"That's because I watch what I eat. I'm a model, remember?"

"If you exercise, you won't get fat. It's obvious you go to the gym."

"Yeah. But I can't be too careful. If you saw my father you'd understand. He's a big guy. Huge, actually."

"And your mom?" Kai asked.

"Tiny."

"Well, there you go. Give yourself a break. Have second helpings sometimes."

A warmth settled in the depths of Dane's chest at Kai's gentle words.

Food did soothe him. He felt less unsure of himself now, less drunk. He eyed the champagne but determined that tonight there would be no more alcohol introduced to his system.

The room no longer seemed cold. Just cool. Adequate. More than adequate. And the view before them, as if all the stars from the sky had fallen upon the darkened land, filled him with a new assurance. Maybe things would work out. Maybe this night was a test and he would swim these waters without drowning, without losing his life.

"Do you do this a lot?"

"Huh?" Kai was chewing.

"Bring guys to penthouse suites. Have your way."

148

Kai grinned. "What do you think?"

Dane said, "I don't know what to think."

Kai lowered his gaze. His eyelashes made those familiar, beautiful lacy shadows on his cheeks. "Yeah. I guess you don't."

He looked so innocent in that moment. That boy who had hidden behind his hair. Who had been the butt of teasing, jokes, bullying. And Dane had watched, or not-watched, and said nothing. Done nothing.

I'm a dick.

So he ate the steak. And the salad. And the cobbler. It was all wonderful. Hot. Fresh. And a gift from Kai. So even if this was a casual affair, he was being treated well.

But before they did anything, he would need a toothbrush after all this food.

They took turns in the bathroom which was designed all in white fixtures with black walls. Dane found a toothbrush with a hot pink handle, packaged for use by the customer of course. Another with a green handle lay on the countertop for Kai.

He looked himself over. His sky blue eyes should have been red at the edges from all the whiskey, but they were clear. His hair, however, was a mess. Hanks of dark brown curved about his face. He pushed it back until it swayed to one side, brushing the edges of his shoulder. Shorter bangs feathered haphazard along his forehead, glinting black when the light hit them. His hair was an asset, thick and glossy. Whenever he had it styled for shoots, the stylists raved over it, calling him lucky.

He looked good, but he didn't want that to be why someone was with him.

Kai was different, though. No matter why Kai had crushed on him in high school, even if it was for the looks, Dane still wanted him. He wanted Kai for himself. That was that. Uneasy, still, he could only hope Kai might like him back. In more than just a memory of a crush, and a great first date and sleep-over.

When he came out of the bathroom, Kai was rolling the dinner things to the door. He opened it, pushed them out, and left the cart in the hall. Then without a word he entered the bathroom, leaving Dane staring at the view again.

He felt hot again. He placed his forehead against the cool glass, watching as a light arched over the city, blinking red on one side. A plane. Everything glimmered. Looked clean. Un-smogged. Night was when the city was most beautiful.

He did not hear Kai come out of the bathroom or walk up behind him. But suddenly a hand was in his, barely touching, not clasping, just there.

It might have been better if the touch had been forward, more forceful. This gentleness made it worse. It made it mean something. It made this night more tentative, as if it wasn't already. More like a risk.

A risk for his heart.

Dane turned.

Kai's hand left his. Both arms rose up. He placed his hands on the sides of Dane's face, pushing back, fingertips edging into his scalp, combing. "All that hair," Kai said softly. "It gets in the way of your face."

"You used to hide behind your hair."

"You remember?"

"Of course." But Dane hadn't remembered much until this past day when he'd had time to think back, to recall the days he had ignored Erik's nefarious antics as long as he got to hang with the "in" crowd.

Kai's breath smelled of mint toothpaste. He leaned in.

Their lips brushed.

Dane could not keep his hands from circling Kai's waist, moving up and down.

They stood before the city and the kiss merged them, growing hot, powerful. It was as if his lips melted into Kai's.

150

His tongue tasted minty freshness, but also Kai's warmth and intensity like a pulse as their tongues danced and their mouths sought essences of pleasure. But also something more.

Did Kai feel it, too? It had to be. Kai had come to him. Kai had found him when Dane had been unable to contact Kai. In less than a day.

When they broke apart, they were both breathing hard.

Dane surprised himself by being the one to lead them up the three steps to the chrome-framed, bedroom loft.

It felt strange to have the curtains open on the giant windows. But this high up there was no one to see them. Maybe a satellite could take pictures. Or a drone. Right now Dane didn't care. He liked being surrounded by the night and all its star-glitter with this man in his arms.

Kai sat back on the bed, already undoing his shirt. Dane stood over him, losing the jacket as it slid with a shushing sound to the floor. He rescued his phone and set it on the nightstand.

Kai had left his jacket by their dinner table. All he had was his shirt, his trousers, his shoes and socks.

They disrobed in a hurry, which was good, but not. Dane wanted to take his time with Kai. He didn't want this to be like his other lost encounters with men, decidedly disappointing, over too quickly with Dane not returning calls after only a few dates.

Dane realized he was picky. Maybe even a prude. He had been waiting for fireworks, but also a disbeliever in true love. Until Kai.

Kai moved further back on the bed, naked now, beautifully aroused, his skin golden and soft-looking but lean, showing youthful muscle. His cock was pretty, gold-sheathed with a pink tip that looked like, well, something too sweet and too scrumptious to resist. The perfect balls nestled lovingly against the crack of his ass.

Dane's body tingled all over. Despite all the whiskey, he grew hard fast. First the kiss had undone him. Then seeing Kai naked and leaning against soft pillows. It was as if he was in a dream. He had worried he might have performance anxiety after the whiskey. But he'd had time to decompress, coffee, food. Fuel. It was all good. His body felt good. Firm and young with no resistance to the man he wanted as a lover. Ready for anything.

With no further preliminaries, he bent and ran his hands up the insides of Kai's thighs. Where the gold hairs on the tops of his thighs glimmered, on the soft insides there was no hair except a few strays where Dane touched. The skin was like down. Dane bent and kissed one thigh and then the other.

Kai's body squirmed. He let out a yelp.

Dane smiled. Licked the soft flesh, nipping, kissing where his nips left fleeting pink marks, moving from one leg to the other. Kai could not keep his legs still. He brought his knees up, grabbing for Dane. Dane avoided him, moving his hands slowly up to Kai's hips, avoiding his pretty cock and petting the flat stomach in lazy circles.

Kai groaned. "I want to feel you against me." He reached up, grabbing Dane's shoulders, pulling him down.

Dane finally matched their bodies together, a glorious rubbing of skin, heat, hardness, and Kai's arms pulled him close.

It was lovely. But that thought rankled. This was intimate. This was more deserving of hearth and home. Not a stranger encounter, as Kai had put it, even if it was a nice hotel.

Pushing his errant thoughts aside, Dane kissed Kai as Kai's hands scooped through his hair, pulling lightly.

Kai turned his head. "So soft," he murmured. "So soft."

Dane put his hand on the back of Kai's neck and forced him to kiss him again. Kai went willingly into the kiss, holding Dane's head as their bodies undulated together.

Dane lost himself in a whirl of pleasure, his vision spinning. He needed this man. He wanted this man. He didn't know why. But it was as real as rain in his favorite autumn season, this man who lived on a rolling green hill surrounded by green live oak, brown eucalyptus, purple jacaranda, pink bougainvillea. It was too fantastic not to be real. Too wonderful.

It had to be real for Kai, too. But Dane couldn't know for sure in a damned hotel room. But he would make the best of it for now because this was too damn good to stop. Too damn wonderful.

His chest ached. He kissed Kai harder. Kai was into it, straining upward. Their cocks rubbed against hips, abdomens, each other.

Kai came up strong this time, rolling Dane over onto his back. Before Dane could get his bearings, Kai was licking his neck, then on down to his chest. He took a pale brown nipple into his mouth and sucked. The sensation went straight to Dane's groin.

Dane arched up, his cock waving, thrumming against his abdomen, begging to be stroked.

Slowly, Kai worked his way from one nipple to the other, giving both undivided attention before moving downward. He was kind and tender, fingers grazing Dane's balls, rubbing, but still avoiding his erection.

Seeing that golden head move lower, Dane almost came without being touched. Finally, Kai grasped him. There. Right there. Hands moving from his balls to the base of his shaft, supporting his heavy erection so it pointed straight up. Then Kai lowered his mouth to him, taking first the tip against his lips, gently suckling, and then more.

Dane gasped. "Fuck. Oh fuck." It was so good. He had been needing this all day. Dreaming of it. Kai's hot, hungry mouth. The way it moved up and down his length reverently, the way he milked him to utter euphoria.

"I can't," he gasped. "I can't hold on."

Kai took his mouth away. Damn him. "You can."

"Please," Dane begged, thrusting his hips up.

The mouth returned. So good. So hot and wet. He wanted to come this way. He could do this all night. He knew he could.

Kai seemed to be of the same mind. He sucked harder, hand circling the base of his shaft, pulling it as he sucked, as his mouth tugged and the soft lips caressed and the tongue teased the underside. Up and down.

Dane could not hold back.

He came with a yell. Flung one hand over his eyes, the other arm hugging his own chest. He thrust up again and came again, his cock pulsing as if it would never stop. Kai kept sucking.

Finally, Dane grew tender and sat up, laughing softly, pulling Kai into a kiss. "Stop." He kissed him. "Give me a minute." He kissed him again.

When he caught his breath and the kissing grew more languid, he toppled Kai onto his back and returned the favor, giving focused attention to his chest and nipples, to his belly, and again caressing the soft inner thighs.

Kai said, "Dane! Fuck!"

So Dane took pity and sucked the tip of his pretty pink head into his mouth.

Kai thrashed.

Dane sucked harder, taking more into his mouth. He caressed the soft flesh of the balls, rolling the roundness against his palm.

Kai was a heap of groaning, growling, arching flesh when Dane was through with him, cock throbbing, shooting against the back of his throat. Dane swallowed the tartness, barely tasting it, liking only that it was Kai who was taking so much pleasure from him. Kai who was so pleasing to him, and who, he now knew, he was falling in love with.

Side by side, they kissed a little more, pausing often to catch their breaths.

Dane stroked Kai's flank, loving the feel. He let his fingers stroll to the buttocks, to the curve and softness, and Kai curled into him more, face at his neck, licking lazily.

They dozed together for maybe fifteen minutes, everything shadowy, serene, the reflections of the city lights making the windows scintillate. There was no need for talk. The silence was not awkward. There was only the warmth between them, their skin touching at knee, hip, chest. Hands caressing. The tart scent of arousal. Faint sweetness of lingering cologne. Mint on the lips. The saltiness of love-damp skin. Beneath them, the sheets smelled of fresh laundering, like sweet dawn wind.

Dane opened his eyes from a dream of spinning, starry skies.

Kai, green-eyed and looking slightly feral, gazed back. Dane could read him clear. Kai wanted to do it again. Dane reached out to Kai's waist, brushing his palm down, down, then coming up between their bodies to feel Kai's stiffness.

Smile met smile. For the first time. Kai. Smiled.

Dane felt himself harden, the familiar thrill and rush of blood, the pooling pleasure in his belly, on the backs of his thighs, in his balls. Just the thought of that now smiling mouth had him. Caught and cornered. Helpless. Hopeless before that tilted face, those new spring eyes. How he wanted Kai.

Together they moved on the bed, wrinkling the spread. Already the black part of the bedspread had fallen to the floor. Now the white comforter joined it. Along with a couple of body pillows.

First Kai was on top, then Dane. Then Kai again.

It was all so terrific. Being with Kai. Dane had never known this feeling before.

Kai's hands roamed to Dane's buttocks, stroking, giving little pats and squeezes. Dane loved it. Kai's fingers delved shyly toward his crack, gentle and undemanding.

Dane relaxed into Kai's body, cheek pressed to Kai's chest, focusing on the hands massaging his ass, letting his body float and his breathing become shallow.

Finally, kissing his cheek sweetly, Kai reached over Dane, pressing his body into the side of Dane's face. Dane heard a rustling. After a few seconds, Kai moved back onto his side facing Dane.

Dane looked between them where Kai held a couple of condoms and a bottle of lube.

Suddenly, something in Dane's chest caught hard and held, growing more and more tense until there was no small amount of pain. He breathed in hard. Winced. He wanted Kai. Oh how he wanted Kai.

But—

"What is that?" He heard himself almost stammer. His voice was aflutter.

Kai's eyebrows rose. "I want you. That's what that is."

Dane swallowed hard. He wanted Kai, too. So much.

"This hotel provides everything, don't they?"

"I told you I called ahead."

"You planned this?" Dane sat up and drew his knees to his chest. His erection still yearned. But his chest pounded. He knew anxiety when he felt it. He'd had it as a kid after his parents had divorced.

But this wasn't about divorce. It wasn't even about fucking. It was about fucking Kai. He didn't want that. Of course he did want it, but not like this.

Kai sat up and put a hand on Dane's shoulder. "Okay?" he asked.

"No, not okay." He blinked a little too rapidly.

"All right. I'm cool. I'm sorry if I'm rushing things."

Dane looked at him then, eyebrow raised. "Seriously? You think we're rushing things? We're in a hotel. I thought this was casual. You made it casual. I don't do—that—as casual." In honesty, he'd never done *that*, but he wasn't going to say it out loud. Especially not now.

156

"I said all right." Kai's voice came out clipped, rushed. Maybe even a little desperate. His smile was all gone.

The awkwardness Dane wanted to avoid all evening returned full force. There had been beauty and pleasure and a rush so great he could not describe it in a hundred years. He had *felt* something. A power beyond his own being. A sharing. A connection. An intimacy that settled into him like waves of warm water but also with a crashing force that made him want to laugh and run and grab Kai and hold him with all his strength. He'd had all that with Kai.

So why was he suddenly being contrary? Recalcitrant?

His body trembled within, but not from excitement now. It was fear. He might be on his way to being a top model posing in his underwear on billboards and buses, but he was not used to revealing himself, the truth within. His bared soul like a burning star for all to see. Or not all. Just one man. The one man he was falling in love with.

It was too much. Too risky. For what if Kai was not falling in love with him? It all seemed too planned, too pat.

"I need to leave," he said huskily.

"What? Why? You said you had nothing planned tomorrow."

"I forgot I have a shoot at nine," Dane lied. He didn't look at Kai as he scooted to the foot of the bed and looked about for his clothes. The lights from the window behind him threw shadows onto the floor. His own looked elongated, sinister.

Dane heard Kai beginning to breathe a little harder. He ignored it.

Kai said, "Dane, don't—"

"I have to go."

"You don't. I'm sorry. I'm sorry you don't like the room, I'm sorry if you—"

"Don't apologize. This was great. Really great." Heart beating far too fast, Dane still did not look over his shoulder. When he felt the bed move as if Kai were coming closer, he stood and gathered his clothes and shoes, heading straight down the three steps and to the bathroom.

As he dressed, he refused to look at himself in the mirror. He thought he heard Kai moving around the hotel room.

For a minute, after everything was in place, shirt tucked, shoes on, he closed his eyes and forced deep, even breaths. He was leaving a man in the middle of the night whom he cared about. He was a dick. There was nothing else to be said.

But his chest still ached. Badly. He couldn't do this. This one most intimate thing. Not with Kai in a hotel room. Not like this. And he didn't know how to deal with it any other way than to leave. To start over, maybe. Another day.

He needed to leave or he was afraid he would no longer be able to breathe. Something was happening to him. He needed a bit of time to sort through it, that was all.

But he knew Kai would not understand. And why should he? That first night Kai had rejected Dane and Dane had not understood.

But his decision was made. If he could just get out of the hotel, go home, try to sleep, maybe the ache would go away. Maybe he could stop being fucking freaked out. Not by Kai, but by his own heart.

When he opened the bathroom door, he expected to see Kai standing just outside it. He wasn't.

Dane looked about the room. Kai stood, fully dressed, by the big windows to the right of the loft.

The night filled the windows with a blackness never ending. Kai was all brown and bronze against that dimness, shoulders back, hands clasped behind his back as if nothing had happened. As if they hadn't just had fantastic sex in a big, plush bed overlooking the Los Angeles light-spill and its surrounding suburbs and cities.

But no, they hadn't had sex. They'd made love. Dane was sure of that now. And that was why this was so very hard.

Dane turned away. Took a step toward the door.

"Before you leave, at least talk to me. Tell me what you're thinking."

Dane said, "I can't." He went across the hard tile to the door and opened it.

"Please don't leave," Kai said.

Dane stepped out.

"Please."

Dane closed the door.

Chapter Fifteen

In the lobby, the lights were garish and hurt his eyes. Dane went to the front desk and asked for a taxi. One was already waiting and they pointed him toward it.

He got in and told the driver where he lived. Then he sat back and let the vehicle carry him away.

He sat for long minutes not thinking. Then a thought came. *What have you done?*

His answer: *Saved my heart.*

Another part of his mind said: *No. You are killing it.*

He knew both sides had valid opinions and reasons for their stand. Any time a person began to fall in love, they put their hearts in danger. But any time a person denied the love they deserved, they also threatened their heart.

Damn it. This was supposed to be his year. He was on the verge of being a top model. He'd get offers for movie parts, then. And TV guest spots. His agent could raise his booking rates. He'd be set for life if and when he got too old to be appealing as a mere model.

But now there was Bjin. And Kai. And a feeling as if he was standing on the edge of a sandstone cliff.

The driver interrupted his reverie. "There's a limo following us."

Dane looked over his shoulder, saw two bright white headlights that stood out from the other cars on the freeway."

"You think?" Dane asked. Surely Kai had not had time to call his limo driver and be so close to them on the freeway.

"It's been close since leaving the hotel."

Dane rubbed at his tired face with both hands, pressing his fingers to his eyes. He let out a short laugh. Kai. His very own stalker since the tenth grade. He'd probably called the limo as soon as Dane had entered the bathroom.

"Yeah," Dane said to the driver. "He's sorta stalking me."

"Really? Should I call the police?"

"Naw. Don't speed, either. I can handle him. He's not a stranger. He's a friend."

"Oh. You scared me for a minute there."

"I just didn't want to talk to him right now."

"Well," the driver said amicably, "it seems he wants to talk to you."

Dane's stomach did a flip. "Yeah. He does."

The thought made him feel both good and bad. Kai was pursuing him, but Kai was unsure. Which was why he'd booked the hotel. That meant Kai wanted him. That was good. But did Kai want to commit? If not, he couldn't blame him, but Dane was not prepared to just play. He was feeling too much, too fast. It wasn't how he did things in his life. And he was still hurt about the hotel thing. He'd made it clear to Kai he didn't go to hotels with men, but Kai had said nothing and let him drink the whiskey to relax. Simply, Dane was overwhelmed. His mind reeled.

It was past midnight, the evening in full bloom. Car lights and streetlights flashed gold with a blue edge on the cab windows. If Dane unfocused his eyes, the glass looked shattered. Broken. He blinked. Glanced over his shoulder again. He could see the limo's outline behind them, a sleek, imposing presence.

Funny. He could still taste whiskey in the back of his throat. And feel the electricity of Kai pressed against him in the plush, hotel bed. At the thought, he became instantly aroused again.

From one city to another, the cab drove. From darkness to darkness glistening with nightlights. Dane did not live too far from Los Angeles, but he did not live directly in the city. About fifteen minutes away, barring traffic.

Trees silhouetted against the night sky moved by like billows of smoke. The cab took the next off-ramp. A posh neighborhood. Slicker than most. Between poverty and the multi-rich. His condo gave him space and peace.

But not as nice as a house on an autumn hill surrounded by bougainvillea and hundred year oaks.

The cab pulled up to the front entrance where a wrought-iron gate barred stone steps leading up to Dane's front door. He might have wished for bougainvillea framing that gate. Instead, he had oleander put there by the homeowners association. Technically, he had no yard.

Dane paid the cab driver, giving him an enormous tip, and hurried through the gate. Just as he got to his door, and the cab took off, he saw the limo pull around the corner. Dane got his key in the lock, opened his door and stepped inside. He closed the door behind him without looking back.

For a moment he stood in the foyer. The air poured over him, cool, smelling of home, and he breathed deep. He flung his house keys into an aquamarine glass bowl on a stand by the door and entered his living room. The kitchen counter gleamed along one side. He headed that way, thinking to grab himself a bottle of water. Or maybe he'd just lean against the counter and sob.

His eye caught something white on the countertop. The mug with the dragonfly handle. Kai had meant for him to keep it. Even then, Kai had begun to make connections. Little hooks into him.

Then why the hotel?

Dane turned and went to his living room window. The thick, beige curtains were shut, but he peeked out along one side.

The limo looked sleek along the curb out front, its lights dimmed until only the yellow parking lights showed like beast's eyes peering from the dark. He could hear the hum of it. So it wasn't completely parked… or stopped. It was sort of hovering. Dane could see no movement from within.

His eyes tracked the walkway. The gate was closed. He pushed his forehead against the glass, trying to see the front steps that led to his door. That was when he saw the black shoes, the bent knees, and a guy sitting there fiddling with his phone, dark blond head bent forward. The porch light glinting silver in the loose, non-hair-sprayed locks. They threatened to take over his face, reminding Dane again of the cowering fourteen year-old who'd been the victim of a bully.

This man no longer cowered. He sat on the front step like he lived there. Casual and still. Not even a flicker of nerves showed. And that tilt to his head. He had to have trained himself to do that, to make himself never again look like the hang-dog victim of harsh childhood years.

Dane stood back from his curtains. He rested his shoulder against the wall.

Kai. Fuck.

How could Dane resist?

The night before, it had been Dane sitting on Kai's front porch steps. Strange how life ran in such unpredictable circles.

It was nearly one a.m. now. Dane's fists closed, opened, closed again. He knew what he wanted. But he had to gear himself up for it.

Why was this so hard? It should be exciting to fall for someone. A thrill. But Dane was afraid. More, his heart was afraid. He would survive it if Kai went away. But his heart would hate the pain. So much.

Sighing hard, he moved through his living room, passing by the kitchen counter where the mug still sat, white and gleaming.

Kai did not want to let go. He had not wanted to even when he'd kicked Dane out, before they'd taken their walk to the stand of oaks, before they'd gone back to Kai's bedroom and spent the night together.

Dane did not want to let go, either.

Dane needed to remember this.

He turned toward the front door.

When he opened it and walked out to the first step, Kai didn't even look up. Asshole.

"What are you doing?" Dane asked.

"Reading."

"No, I mean what are you doing on my porch?"

"Reading."

Dane made a guttural sound of protest. This didn't have to be so difficult. "Reading what?"

"About Bjin. Look at him. He says he admires you, but that's really him competing with you. Name-dropping. Leaning on your fame. You see that, don't you?"

"I don't care." He didn't want to hear about Bjin. Was Kai trying to piss him off more?

"You should care, Dane. He's coming right up underneath you to topple your success, steal it. It's the game. It's business. If you fail to see—to see this happening, to see Bjin playing you—you lose."

Dane thought about Kai's choice of words. He'd said "to see" several times. It was important to him. To his situation. To be seen. To see. To look around the immediate vicinity and see what was happening right under one's nose.

Dane had failed Kai in that sense. When they were teenagers. And that had hurt Kai. Now Kai had decided Dane was looking the other way again, to the detriment of his own career.

"Okay, I see him. Bjin. He's a little shit with fancy looks and a fancy name. I get it. I don't know what to do about it, but I get it."

Dane took a step forward and sat next to Kai, who was still fiddling with his phone. Dane saw Bjin's photo scroll by several times. Small words followed. Articles. Interviews. All about the up-and-coming boy model who was already getting contracts with the hottest designers in the world.

Kai said, as if casually discussing the weather, "He knows nothing. Of the world. Of modeling. Of grace or sophistication. If a child can do the job the best for the clients, so be it, but I say no. Not for the clients with the big ticket items. Not for the real designers, the artists."

164

It was almost the same thing Terry had said to him earlier in the evening.

"What do you know of the industry of modeling?"

Kai glanced up, then down again. "Nothing. But I know business. He's sixteen. He doesn't even know what it's like to keep promises yet. He won't show up on time, or if he does his mom will be with him. He'll only be able to work short days. He'll whine in bad weather and look stiff everywhere he shouldn't, and flaccid everywhere he should look stiff. For now, those underwear ads are out of his range. He's got nothing on you. You need to know this."

Dane laughed. This was Kai's way of communicating praise but at the same time disapproval that Dane turned away or ran when things got tough. Dane decided, right then, he liked even this part of Kai. A lot.

Kai looked at him again, green eyes flashing. "It's not funny. It's a game, yes, but you need to play it right. You tell the press how flattered you are that Bjin admires you, that he will one day be great, too, with maturity and experience. You make him look like a beginner while saying nothing bad, nothing wrong. They'll eat it up."

Again, Dane laughed quietly.

"Hey," Kai said. "I'm giving you business advice here. It's important. I'll make an app for you. One that follows Bjin so you can keep up."

"I don't want to follow Bjin."

"This is important to your career," Kai protested.

Dane nodded. "I know it is."

"But tonight you were off. I saw you with the press, the fans, the paparazzi. Why?"

"Because." Dane paused, taking a breath. "Because tonight I couldn't see all that."

"Why not?"

"Because tonight all I could see—everywhere I looked, every time I closed my eyes—was you."

The phone in Kai's hand tilted, started to fall.

Dane reached out and caught it. Kai looked up, eyebrows raised, his face opening, blooming. Maybe he wasn't aware how beautifully his lips framed the line of his mouth, how his eyes grew big and startled, how the skin of his cheeks pulled taut making him look almost fourteen again, only now he wasn't ducking, hiding, cringing. Now his vulnerability had grace, and a welcome sort of wonder that had, perhaps, been saved all for Dane for so many years. Or at least, surely, these last two nights.

Dane handed him back his phone.

"You—" Kai began. But his mouth stayed slightly open, saying nothing more.

"Do you want to come in?"

"In?" Kai started to smile, tried to stop it by clamping down on his lower lip.

Dane wanted so badly to see him give in to that smile again, as he had only a couple of hours ago.

"Yes. This is me inviting you in. To my home. I know what that means to you. You told me. You showed me when you took me to a hotel instead of your house. But now I'm inviting you. It means something to me, too. So don't fuck with me if you don't mean it back."

"Uh. Yeah. Okay." Kai tried again to suppress his grin. "That was quite a speech. You need to remember the energy behind that for when you talk to the press."

"I don't care about the press right now."

"No?"

"No. The energy behind that speech is all for you. I don't know how to make it plainer than that."

"But you ran out on me." Kai said this quite calmly.

"I was... You're overwhelming to me," Dane admitted. Was he saying too much? Not enough?

"I know. I rushed you." Kai shrugged as if it didn't matter. Then he said, gruffly, "Sorry."

Dane said, "You don't have to apologize. It's just the formality wasn't... isn't my thing. And not what I dreamed of for my first time." He gulped. Too much?

Kai blinked, lips pressed tight. He shook his head. "Well, fuck, Dane, why didn't you say so in the first place instead of running?"

Dane felt a smile slowly start to form around his heart. Kai's response was perfect.

Dane said, "Because I'm an idiot?"

"No. You're not. Maybe I am this time around."

"I don't think that at all." Dane watched Kai's whole pose change to a more relaxed demeanor.

Dane stood, reaching out one hand. "Come on. I'll make us some coffee. I have this lovely white mug I've been wanting to use. With a dragonfly handle."

Kai stood. He did not take Dane's hand. "Hmm. Ben gave that to you, did he?"

"On your instructions."

"He said that?"

"Yes. Why, did he lie?"

"I didn't say that." Kai waved to the limo. With a deep purr, it rolled away, the tires crunching against the asphalt. The night air mixed with the scent of gasoline, exhaust, and Kai's sweetness.

The cologne scent of him.

And Dane thought: *It's all my fault that Kai's skittish around me. I didn't see him years ago. When he had his crush. Now? I won't make the same mistake twice.*

Chapter Sixteen

He went into the kitchen when what he really wanted to do was go straight to the bedroom.

Dane put the grounds in the coffee maker and poured in the water. He switched it to *on*. He had a feeling as if he'd run around the block fast without taking a breath. As if he'd plunged straight into a mountain stream and come up right into the blazing heat of summer.

A summer called Kai.

He turned, seeing Kai had taken a seat at the counter on one of the high stools.

The silence between them stretched to awkward. Dane said, "So, you like dragonflies."

Kai said, "In high school you always wore this t-shirt. It had a spattered look, white, blue, green on a black background. And a dragonfly on the front."

Dane started to shake his head. Then he remembered. He'd worn that thing until it was ratty and full of holes. "Seriously, I loved that shirt. I'd forgotten until now."

"So now you know I was completely crazy."

Dane blinked. Smiling wide at the realization. The dragonflies were because of him. All for him. It was both strange and wonderful at the same time. "Yeah. And creepy," he said with a gentle laugh, carefully gauging Kai's reaction.

"Completely. I am embarrassed, don't get me wrong. I grew up. I focused on my life. My career. And trying not being a total nerd. I may have stopped stalking you, but I never stopped collecting dragonflies. I only noticed you again after the billboards. About two weeks ago. Of course I looked you up. Natural curiosity. That's not stalking."

"No," Dane said good-naturedly. "I don't mean to sound conceited, but I figure half our high school class, if they remembered me, started searching for me on the Internet once those underwear ads came out. "

"I may have held a grudge, but I never thought you were conceited. You were just—perfect. Still are."

"Shut up." Heat sparked into Dane's cheeks.

"It's a fact. But sorry if I made you uncomfortable. You invited me in. We gotta get over this discomfort."

"I wasn't perfect, Kai. I'm still not. I ignored you. You were right to hold a grudge, I guess. I didn't see you. And I should have."

The coffee maker started making bubbly noises. Dark roast scent filled the air. Dane got out a black mug that said, "Humbug" on it for Kai. He was determined to use the white one with the dragonfly handle for himself. He got out the cream, and his decanter of sugar and two spoons.

The activity gave him something to do, but Kai had put away his phone, and now he was nervously scratching at his chest, pushing back his hair, rubbing his fingertips against the smooth countertop. A couple of times, he looked as if he wanted to say something and stopped himself. His throat muscles moved. Dane saw a tiny pink mark against the side of Kai's throat where he'd kissed him only an hour or so ago, sucking in a little on the skin. His body became aroused at the memory, arms and legs going cool, then hot.

Kai opened his mouth to speak. Closed it.

Dane leaned on the counter trying not to look directly at him, but peripherally watching the way Kai shifted, took a breath, licked his lips. He could not imagine losing this man. After only two nights, he felt such a rush at the thought of being with him he suddenly forgot why he'd run from the hotel in the first place.

Kai finally spoke. "I want to say I'm sorry again."

For a moment, Dane was confused. "You don't—"

Kai held up his hand to stop him and continued. "I'm not usually so forceful. I was trying to be cool, I guess. In charge. It's a thing I have now, with my business and all. Compensation maybe for my mousy childhood."

So now they were going to talk about the condom. The lube. Upping the game. All the things that had made Dane panic.

But it was just the two of them and a percolating pot of coffee now. And Dane was in his home, on familiar footing, feeling more comfortable. His arousal increased. He had to ask himself why he'd been mad. Afraid. It was all like a dream, that hotel, the black and white bed, the spill of lights over the endless land of L.A. county. Kai in his arms.

Kai said, "I had no idea you'd never—that it was going to be your first time. For, um, for that." He didn't say "anal sex" but he didn't have to. They both knew what he was talking about.

Dane gulped.

The coffee was nearly done. Dane took the mugs and poured some into each. He handed the humbug mug to Kai. Kai put his hand on it, breathing in as the steam rose into his face.

Kai said, almost a whisper. "I had no idea—"

"I want it." Dane did not look up as he poured cream into his cup. He marveled that his hands weren't shaking. He felt Kai's gaze on him. "With you," Dane finished, voice rough, low.

"You don't have to—" Kai began.

Dane interrupted again. "Shh! You talk too much. Okay?"

Kai pressed his lips tight. Made a funny face.

Dane stirred sugar into his coffee. "I invited you into my home. It's not casual for me anymore. Not after our car chase"

"I didn't chase you." Kai gave a nervous chuckle.

Dane ignored the statement. "But if you say you don't feel the same, then I'm not inviting you any further. Not into my bedroom." *Not into my heart.*

170

Kai took a spoon, scooped some sugar onto it, brought it to his mug. Dane couldn't be more pleased to see a trail of white granules spill everywhere but into the cup. Kai had chinks in his armor. Finally!

Kai said, "I've been with guys, but not like that, either. I haven't wanted to. Until now."

Dane felt like he couldn't breathe. It passed in a second. "Okay, then." He lifted the white mug with the pretty handle to his lips and blew on the hot liquid.

Kai kept touching his own mug but did not lift it. He was gazing into it as if it were some oracle telling him what to do. "So, now you know this isn't casual for me, either," he said. "Do you want a ring or something?"

Dane's eyes stung for a moment, in a sweet way. He cleared his throat. Played along. "Platinum. Diamond-encrusted."

"Of course," Kai replied, right on cue.

Dane took a sip of his coffee. It burned the tip of his tongue. He blew on it again. Trying to distract himself. His cock pulsed, shifting hard against his trousers. He wanted the taste of Kai again. Not coffee. Not words. Taste, touch, texture, scent.

Dane took a deep breath and turned away from the counter. "I'm going to turn down my bed. Follow me in about twenty seconds. If you want, bring the coffee with you."

Chapter Seventeen

Dane left his own drink steaming on the counter, and the beautiful white mug shone in the kitchen's low glow.

When he entered his bedroom, he turned on the red glass lamp on his nightstand. It gave out enough light to see, but muted. He opened the nightstand drawer and took out a bottle of lube. Brand new. Never used. He'd been saving this one, strawberry scented, for a special occasion. This was it.

He made good on his word. He turned down the covers of his bed on both sides, neatly, evenly. He'd never done that for a lover before. Never thought to. But right now he didn't know what else to do. He was so hot. So hungry again for Kai.

It was almost 1:30 now. Dane parted the white curtains and opened the window a few inches, letting in fresh air. The neighborhood silence drifted in.

There was a slight breeze, and the prickly scent of juniper. He glanced out toward the back of the complex where he could see a tall jacaranda, two palm trees, and low oleander bushes with white and pink and purple blooms. They glowed beneath the distant parking lot's sodium lamps. Some of the windows of the surrounding condos gave off a tawny light, but most were dark. It was late. Most humans were sleeping now.

Dane heard a footstep on soft carpet, and the drag of his bedroom door over the thick pile. He turned. Kai stood in the doorway, a lock of flaxen hair falling against the edge of his cheekbone, green eyes wide and round. He did not look like the CEO of a multi-million dollar company right now. Still, his head tilted back in his familiar stance of assuredness. But he was open. More open than Dane had ever seen him.

Dane let the curtain fall closed. It billowed slightly in the autumn breeze.

He was ready for this. He was.

Kai came into the room, shrugging his shoulders back with a sophistication that lent itself to grace and a kind of innocence that was streamlined but sweet. He'd built an empire. But he was still just Kai.

Dane could see the bulge at the center of Kai's trousers. It was a relief to see that.

Dane moved to the edge of the bed and sat, watching him. Kai came forward until he stood only a inch from Dane's bent knees.

Up close, Kai's eyes looked a little watery. "I have a confession."

Dane waited, eyebrows raised.

"I think I've fantasized this moment about a thousand and ninety-nine times."

Dane said, "Then how will I ever measure up to your dreams?"

"You already exceed them."

Dane's body heated all over. There was that sting again in his eyes at Kai's admission. He blinked it back and reached out. Kai sort of fell against him and Dane let himself go back until he was flat on the bed, Kai over him, and everything was right again. So right.

He heard Kai let out a groan. Felt his erection pressed to his own through their clothing. Smelled again that expensive cologne, like midnight dew with a hint of autumn smokiness.

Their lips found each other. Dane's heart squeezed inside his chest. Things had never felt this natural, this compatible in bed before. He raised his arms around Kai's shoulders, pulling him in tighter.

Kai breathed against his mouth. "I'll have to order the ring. It might take awhile."

"Shut. Up." Dane found his lips again, such relenting softness, putting a stop to more words.

Kai's hands ran up and down his sides. Dane thrust against him, wanting to feel more of that hardness between the legs, more of Kai.

Their clothes were in the way. Kai leaned up and Dane began undoing the buttons on his shirt for the second time that night.

Straddling Dane's thighs, Kai balanced until he could begin to undo Dane's shirt as well. They were a tangle of arms and hands, bumping, fumbling. It wouldn't do.

Dane sat all the way up, scooting back, undoing his own shirt in seconds and flinging it away. Kai did the same, then stood and got rid of his trousers in a desperate flourish. His erection bobbed up, nearly slapping his abdomen. So lovely with that shiny pink tip, the whole of it surrounded by short blond curls. His narrow hips made the curve of his ass look tighter, and showed off the lean muscles of his thighs.

Dane loved everything about Kai's body. He wanted to feel him again.

Quickly, he pushed his trousers down, taking his shoes off with them, and grabbed him around the waist. Kai moved between his legs and bent to kiss him again. Now their bodies could truly meet, unclothed, no barriers, skin to skin, honest and true.

Kai's cock dragged against Dane's belly. His own was trapped against Kai's thigh. He squirmed to feel some friction from that as Kai took his mouth deeper, tongue thrusting. He tasted smoky and salty, and honey sweet.

After awhile, they fell to their sides, gasping for breath, nipping at the flesh of necks, shoulders, pecs. Kai spent a long time sucking on Dane's left nipple, laving it while he caressed his balls with deft fingers.

Taking his time, Kai's hands traveled to Dane's buttocks, massaging closer and closer to the crack. The sensation made Dane's cock throb with need. Kai was the first man he wanted this way. That was why he'd run. He wanted Kai that much. Too much. And also it had been a fucking hotel. He'd vowed early in his adult life never to lose his virginity in a hotel.

Now the last thing he wanted was to run.

"Kai, yes. Yes."

Kai pushed him over and onto his back. Dane lifted his legs, knees bent, so Kai could get more access.

Kai bent down. Dane felt his tongue drag up the underside of his cock as he gently stroked between Dane's crack.

Kai brought his head up, licking the tip of Dane's cock, which grew slicker at the sensation, and said, "Lube."

Dane reached out and felt around for the bottle he'd put on the nightstand. He found it and thrust it at Kai just as Kai sucked the tip of his cock with a sweet, kissing sound.

Much to Dane's disappointment, Kai drew away and took the bottle. He heard the seal break, the cap being unscrewed. Scent blossomed through the air.

"Strawberries?" Kai asked.

"I love strawberries," Dane replied.

"So be it," Kai said, giving a little chuckle.

Dane waited for what seemed a long time but was probably only seconds. Finally, he felt a cool liquid begin to run between his legs and over his balls. Fingers, slick and wet, probed further, touching the entrance to his body, teasing. Dane wanted more, and spread his legs wider, pulling his knees further up.

The mouth returned to his cock, sucking now, making him shiver all over. The finger gently rubbed until he remembered to relax. Next came the tentative finger probe.

Okay, then. He was really going to do this.

Kai probed over and over, gently thrusting. It didn't hurt at all. Then Kai took his mouth from Dane's cock and licked his way up his stomach, giving attention to his nipples again, his neck, his mouth. They kissed as Kai gently stroked him inside.

Dane's body rippled in unchecked pleasure.

Kai pulled back, breath wafting against Dane's cheek. "Tell me you really want this. I want to be sure."

"I really want this. With you. Only you."

Kai sighed. "You have to be sure."

"Damn it, I'm sure."

Kai's erect cock trailed along Dane's hip and belly and thigh as he scooted down in the bed, taking Dane into his mouth again, fingers continuing to lube and stroke at the insides of Dane's ass. It was all too much. Dane wanted it to never end, but he wanted Kai inside him soon. Now.

He thrust up into Kai's mouth as Kai pushed two fingers inside him. Dane held himself back, not ready to come yet. He would have been unable to control himself if they hadn't already had sex at the hotel. Now things were a little easier, less urgent, although the urgency inside him built and built. But it did not crest too soon and for that he was grateful.

Kai took his time, his free hand moving all over Dane's body, stroking him gently as if to calm him. Well, Dane was calm except for wanting to fuck now. He was quite calm aside from the conflagration of excitement, a rapidly beating heart, and being brought to the pinnacle of coming over and over again.

"Please, Kai," he moaned. "I'm ready."

"I'll be the judge," Kai said, licking the head of his cock.

Dane groaned, shoulders lifting as he tried to sit up.

"Relax," Kai said, placing one hand on his chest. "It won't work if you aren't relaxed."

"Did you read that somewhere?"

"Well," Kai said thoughtfully, licking at the head of Dane's cock again. "Yes."

"Fuck that. I'm ready. I want you to do it now."

Kai's fingers continued to tease. It was as if Dane had no voice in the timing of this whatsoever. Kai had already decided the course of action, the when, the how, all of it.

Dane decided to just lie back and enjoy. Over and over, Kai had him nearly cresting to full-fledged pleasure before

176

holding off, letting his tension subside. It was crazy. It was wonderful.

Dane heard a rustling of cellophane. "What's that?" But of course he knew. Dane had not put out condoms. Only lube.

"This?" Kai held up a circle of latex in the dim, pink light.

"Where did you get that?"

"I come prepared. It's the one from the hotel."

Dane reached out. "Can I see?"

Kai held it up. Suddenly, Dane grabbed it and threw it across the bed. It disappeared into the shadows at the other side of the room.

"The fuck?" Kai drew back everything, body, fingers, warmth, touch.

"I don't want it," Dane said.

"What?"

"We're both virgins in this way. I haven't been with anyone since 2016. You?"

"Longer ago than that."

"I trust you," Dane said. He wanted to feel Kai, all Kai, only Kai, skin on skin. He didn't care about anything else right now. And he knew it was safe. Why should he say okay to a fucking condom? He wasn't promiscuous, and anyway he hated them.

"What if I want the condom," Kai said.

"Do you?"

A pause. Then, "You crazy bastard."

"Just put it in me," Dane said, shocked at his explicit audacity. But he had waited long enough. He wanted to feel Kai. He wanted him so badly, this rare connection, and also just to know what it might be like to make love, finally, in this way.

"You crazy beautiful bastard." This time Kai's voice came as a half-whisper, and Kai kissed him gently on the lips as his fingers spread him again and he pressed close, closer. The closest he'd ever been.

Dane felt the tip of Kai's cock touch him right there in the center, the opening to his body.

"Yes," Dane whispered. "Please." He shoved up with his hips to encourage his lover. Kai pushed against him, his oiled cock going astray right up the back of Dane's ass crack.

Dane let out a muffled laugh. "Try again."

They couldn't be perfect their first time. He never expected that. But it was perfect. All of it. Even this. Because he knew now that he loved Kai. And that sweet body was in his arms, warm and firm, and his cock was pushing against him and he loved all of this more than he could ever define.

Kai aimed again, his hands between Dane's legs, fingers feeling for the slick edge of Dane's opening, the tip of his cock probing.

Yes, that's it. That's it.

Kai pushed. He went awry again, but less so and Dane felt himself opening to him anyway, those sweet fingers holding him open, one digit inside as Kai lined up again.

"Go on," Dane said. "Please, oh please."

Kai thrust.

Dane gasped. It was harder than he'd imagined taking him in, yet wonderful after the first raw feeling receded. Kai was only half in but it was amazing. He stayed very still, letting Dane get used to the sensation. Dane decided Kai should be commended on incredible control.

Dane felt his body relax and accept the intruder, the stranger visiting the strange land for the first time. He welcomed it. His body moved and Kai slipped further into him with a definite groan of pleasure.

Dane mirrored that groan and the room echoed with their voices combined in pleasure, a song of pure ecstasy.

"All the way," Dane said, wondering where his voice came from when he could not breathe.

The slip, the slide, the shared warmth and pressure. And then Kai was all the way inside, an intimate touching the likes of which Dane had never known.

"Dane, you feel so—so—oh fuck." Kai began to move.

"Slowly first," Dane gasped.

"Yes."

But he needn't have bothered with those instructions, for it was incredible, Kai sliding inside him back and forth just a little at first, and then, soon, and so amazing, in and out, picking up the tempo. He tried to thrust up with the strokes, partake in the dance, everything getting hotter, slicker, as if the weather had suddenly changed and a hot wind with warm rain blew over them. What a concept. Weather indoors. Mist. Fog. The satiny sounds of their lovemaking.

Kai leaned down and took Dane's mouth again. Dane bucked up, meeting the thrusts.

"Oh," he said into Kai's mouth. "Oh, wow."

"Good?"

Something inside him pulsed to life, tingled as Kai's cock stroked in, out. "Shit!" Dane cried out.

Kai stopped. "What?"

"That's so good. You hit my prostate. Don't stop."

"Oh. Yeah. Good? Okay."

Through it all, Dane could not stop his groans. Every time the tip of Kai's cock hit his prostate, he thought he would explode. His cock felt huge, pulsing with pleasure. He wanted to come. But he wanted this to last.

Kai thrust faster and Dane knew he could not help it. He was on the verge, losing control. But not so far gone that he ignored Dane's cock. His hand wrapped around it, stroking in time with his thrusts.

The milking of his cock along with the sweet sliding inside his ass sent him teetering over the edge. And then he was falling and falling, nothing around him but white stars and fire and the purest ecstasy he'd ever known.

He'd never come so deeply, as if the friction on his prostate and cock combined to make a double orgasm. He had the thought that if he did not survive this, he'd die a happy man.

The cock inside him pulsed. Kai went rigid in his arms even as Dane was losing his reason. But he held onto the man as they both went into the euphoria together.

Distantly, he felt liquid pulsing inside him, hot and sweet, Kai filling him with pleasure, with love. It was a lot. It seemed they would both never stop coming.

For a long time, Dane could not open his eyes. He held Kai tight to him, chest to chest, his legs wrapped about the backs of Kai's thighs. Kai was still inside him, though everything had gone still. He wondered when he finally had the energy to open his eyes what he would see. The world changed? A new reality?

For this—this was earth-shattering.

He felt a nudge against his jaw. Kai's cheek pressed to his.

"Please don't move yet," Dane whispered.

"I won't. Not ever if you don't want me to."

Dane took a deep breath. The sides of his face felt wet at both temples. Was he crying? He didn't remember crying.

"Good," Dane said.

Kai held him until their breathing quieted. Still, he did not move. Finally, Kai raised his hands to Dane's face, framing it, kissing him.

Pulling away, Kai said, "You're the most incredible guy. You know that, right?"

Dane grinned up at him. "When can we do it again?"

Epilogue

Gold lights flashed. Then white. Brighter than the sun. Blinding.

Voices could be heard calling.

"Bjin. Bjin."

Cameras whirring. Coiffed and perfect reporters. Movie stars with lacquered hair and fake smiles. Male and female. Dressed to the nines.

Rapid fire questions. Cameras competing.

Dane heard it all before he stepped away from the limo, before they all turned to him. A flutter of nerves tickled inside his stomach. For courage, as he always did now when he felt the lingering presence of stage fright, he pressed his thumb over the smooth, diamond-encrusted platinum band he wore on his left ring finger. The fear went away.

The voices grew in volume. Moving toward him. "It's Dane Asher. Dane! Dane!"

Dane smiled. Waved. Watched as Bjin slinked off, ignored now that Dane had come onto the red carpet scene. Dane who had taken the modeling world by storm and was now the top male model in the world, fielding movie roles right and left once they figured out he was an actor, too, picking and choosing his shoots from around the world, raking in the bucks.

"Dane, who is that with you?" shouted a reporter from one of the biggest media gossip channels in the USA.

Dane reached back for Kai's hand, pulling him out of the limo behind him.

Kai had insisted on remaining in the background throughout the past year. Unseen. But Dane had requested he come with him tonight for the open Hollywood gala, star-studded and rife with glitz.

He wanted Kai to be seen. He would never forget how he'd once looked away from such an incredible human being. Never forgive himself for not seeing Kai. But now he wanted Kai to know he saw him. And the rest of world would, too.

"This is my husband. Kyle Northwood," said Dane.

Dear Reader:

Thank you for reading *Buying You*. I hope you enjoyed it as much as I did writing it!

If you take the time to review it, even just one line, it would be an enormous help.

If you enjoyed this, you might also enjoy subscribing to my newsletter. I put it out about six times a year to announce new books and upcoming projects, and I always have sales and freebies to offer readers both from myself and other authors I enjoy reading. If you subscribe at the link below, you can get a free copy of my critically acclaimed sci fi mm romance book *Letters to an Android*.

Happy Reading!

Wendy Rathbone

Contact links for Wendy:

Facebook: https://www.facebook.com/wendy.rathbone.3

Blog: http://wendyrathbone.blogspot.com/

Newsletter sign up (you get a free copy of the critically acclaimed "Letters to an Android"): https://www.instafreebie.com/free/3ErH0

About Wendy Rathbone

I love to write. I love words and how they are used to describe beauty, love, and all the things that open us up inside to our true self, our power. Words do that for me. They make me happy. The new moon smiling, the sadness of a fallen feather at dusk, predatory eyes gazing through smoke.

The reason I write romance these days is because the overwhelming power of falling in love (which has been proven to heal even cancer) is a game-changer. It makes sad people instantly happy. It makes bleak reality look sun-warmed and friendly again.

I have written in all genres: sci fi, fantasy, horror, paranormal, contemporary, erotica, romance. My poetry has won awards, publishing contracts, and was recently nominated for a Pushcart. I am a hybrid writer, publishing both indie (under my press name Eye Scry Publications) and with publishers, most recently with Dreamspinner Press.

I keep coming back to romance. Gay romance. Male/male romance. The intensity of it makes my muse soar. It's so much fun!

This is why I write. This is what makes me burn.

All my books are available on Kindle and CreateSpace. Many are in Kindle Unlimited. My most recent bestseller is "The Imposter Prince" which readers could not put down. So if you have the urge, go take a look. See what's on the shelf.

Love to you all!

Wendy Rathbone

The Imposter Prince
Wendy Rathbone

His love for an enemy prince threatens his very life.

Dare does not mind serving the spoiled and cruel Prince Darius. Growing up with him, Dare does everything for Darius including homework, bed play demands, and even doubling for him as the prince grows too paranoid to face even the smallest of crowds.

But everything changes in a single moment when Dare, while posing as Darius, is abducted by the enemy.

A captive in a new and hostile land, Dare meets another prince who seems just as indulged and rotten as Darius—until Dare gets to know him, until they fall in love. Against his will, Dare must continue to play the role of Prince Darius for real, or risk everything: his love, his land, and his very life.

His only chance for survival is to keep a secret from the one he loves, a secret that is also killing him.

A male/male, enemies to lovers novel of mad kings, troubled princes, abduction, fevers, cold dungeons, warm hearths, comfort, wine, and true love.

Cocky Virgin Prince
(of Android City)
Wendy Rathbone

MM romance novella. A human drama on a futuristic backdrop set in an unknown time.

You are about to enter the Exalted Sacred Chamber of Pleasure. You are about to participate in the Rite of Ecstasy. All humans of Android City must go through this rite to honor the body-temple while they are still young and have all their natural human attributes.

But…

You are unwilling, unsure, unhappy, and you are a cocky, defiant prince who hates his life.

Your story began when your one true love left when you were twelve and you barely knew what love was. You never got over it. You named him your number one archenemy. And you have decreed, as Prince Night of Android City, that no one touches your royal ass. No one.

Nevertheless, your father the cyborg king forces you into the Sacred Chamber.

And who should appear after nine years of sorrow, grief and loneliness but your very best friend from childhood. Yes, the one who left you. The one who entered the Academy of Sacred Pleasure to become one of the sexiest and most talented Guides for leading others in the Rite of Ecstasy.

Your number one archenemy. He is a beautiful man now, and you hate him even more than you can imagine. Though by law you cannot leave the Chamber until your virginity is forfeit, you don't care.

You will never let him touch you.

Ganymede: Abducted by the Gods
Wendy Rathbone

My name is Ganymede, and I have been betrayed.

Every boy my age dreams of leaving home to embark on a noble adventure, but never does any boy imagine it happening as it did to me. On the evening of my 18th naming day, when I expected no more than a chalice of wine and a few drunken flirtations to tempt my innocence, I was instead sold by my father to the god, Zeus - not because of anything particular I had ever done or said, but solely because I am considered beautiful among mortals, and my father found more value in a few gold coins than in the well-being of his youngest son.

To be honest, I never believed in the gods, but my lack of belief held no power in Olympus or on Earth. Now under Zeus's influence, I am kept drunk on ambrosia in the sun-lit halls of the immortals, alternately amazed and horrified at the power these beings hold over others, and how darkly they influence the progress of humanity itself. How very much I want to hate Zeus for kidnapping me, and yet he shows me mostly kindness, even on that fateful night when we shared a bed for the first time. Kindness, yes, but also a godly and unyielding refusal to take no for an answer... probably because he could read my ambrosia-fevered curiosity as much as my naive, inexperienced terror. He owns me, after all, just as he owns everything else, so perhaps it never occurred to him that a captive and a slave might not make the best of lovers.

Throughout my time at Olympus - who's to say how long I've been here, for time on Olympus is not the same as that on Earth - the only thing that gives me hope comes to me in dreams and visions. His name is Sable and he is a magnificent shape-shifter in the form of a giant raven. When he first spoke to me in my mind it was with a resonance unlike any I had ever known - his mind and mine sounding a single note together, a song without words, a promise of freedom, a glimpse of some distant but very real possibility of this thing we humans call Love. But now he is silent. Perhaps I dreamed his voice. Perhaps I have finally lost my mind...

www.eyescrypublications.com

Also on Amazon or order from your favorite bookseller.

ZEUS (Conquering His Heart)
WENDY RATHBONE

When I throw the lightning and summon the thunder, it isn't always out of anger, but often from a love so all-consuming it could only be the effect of Eros himself. Yes, he is beautiful. Of course he is. How could he be otherwise, with hair the color of sunlight and white-feathered wings that drape to the floor? And he is as ancient as the myth of time itself, an immortal with powers and glamour beyond my ability to imagine.

He struggles to teach me wisdom, control, strategy, yet I sit here babbling like a child, for all I can think of is how I might try - at least let me try! - to prove myself to him in some way that will cause him to crave my company and my touch, just as I crave his.

I do not yet know how to be a god, for I am only 18 and still just a silly boy who has fallen in love with Love himself, while my father Cronus plots and schemes to lock me in his dungeon and make me his slave forever.

A male/male romance.

PREY
Wendy Rathbone

When the rescued slaves were first brought on board my ship, I saw only the one. The one they called Arcana. And though I realized the others had all suffered similar fates - fearsome torture and erotic conditioning that had estranged them from whoever they had once been - I focused on the one who met my eyes with what could only be interpreted as a defiantly seductive lure, while the others held their gazes downward, at their feet, at the floor, at the past which had shaped them and undoubtedly doomed them to any sort of normal life.

Not so with Arcana. That one had no shame in whatever had happened to him. In that one blinding moment when we saw one another for the first time, I knew he was as brash as he was beautiful, and I knew without any doubt that he had chosen me - though for what dark agenda, I could not have said.

My heart went cold and silent in my chest. My throat was dry. My breathing faltered and I was forever changed.

***

We danced. Captain Mordecai and I. Not any traditional dance, but a dance of power. A battle of yin and yang, light and dark, pleasure and torment. A dangerous dance of right and wrong in a single moment caught outside the tendrils of Time.

It was easy to see the raw and sensual power in that man's gaze. But also the fear. Fear of being seen for who he was behind his carefully-constructed masks. Fear of finally surrendering to the dangerous desires he clearly felt when he looked at me, knowing my past, knowing I had been enslaved by sadistic aliens. Knowing I had not only enjoyed it, but had come to love my master. All the wrong things. So very wrong.

That was when I knew he wanted me. That was when I knew I needed him.

That was when I knew I had him exactly where we both needed him to be.

www.eyescrypublications.com

Also on Amazon or order from your favorite bookseller.

LETTERS TO AN ANDROID
Wendy Rathbone

Cobalt is a created human, vat grown and born adult, with no human rights and indentured to serve others for the duration of his life. Liyan is a young man with wanderlust in his eyes, embarking on a career that takes him to the furthest regions of space. The two become unlikely friends and create a memorable long-distance correspondence. Through Liyan, Cobalt gets to explore the universe, living vicariously through his friend's wave transmissions. A strong bond develops between them that not even the stars can put asunder.

———————————

Now you know an android who writes poetry.

This is all your fault. Did you not read my last wave telling you extracurricular activities for my kind are discouraged? Of course this is harmless and strangely enjoyable and does not necessarily require me to leave the hotel. Pel would not care if I wrote lines of equations or nonsensical juxtaposed words. As long as the act does not bring my mental state into question.

However, in history, poetry is often written by the rebels.

So we can keep this to ourselves.

Let me know about your lieutenant's test.

And to give you peace of mind, I never believed you observed me as anything other than human.

Some people are and always will be hateful bigots. Most people are simply uncomfortable in speaking to "property." And anyway, friendship, like poetry, is also discouraged.

Your friend,
Cobalt

SCOUNDREL
Wendy Rathbone

Antares is a willing sex slave, trained in the harems of Anada since the age of 18, and owned by a wealthy master who spoils his slaves. But all that changes when Empire soldiers invade Antares' world and he is taken away from the only life he's ever known.

In a colonized galaxy where starships are as common as houseflies, and a dark Empire seeks to control thousands of civilized worlds, there are those who fall through the cracks and refuse to be conquered, including the pirate, Slate, and his crew.

Out in the darkness of the unknown, among Empire soldiers and scoundrels, will bad fates befall Antares and his fellow captive companions?

Will Slate finally find the love he's been looking for his whole life?

Can Slate and Antares ever see eye to eye?

A male/male romance to end all male/male romances!

www.eyescrypublications.com
Also on Amazon or
order from your favorite bookseller.

THE FOUNDLING
Wendy Rathbone

Diego is a powerful man with a tragic past. Out on the expansive ocean in his private yacht, he discovers a beautiful and mysterious man adrift on a raft, near death. The bond that forms between them in the aftermath of Alec's rescue is one of fierce passion, though lacking in trust. Can they make it work, or will Alec's amnesia bring forth secrets so disturbing as to tear them apart? A passionately erotic love story of desire and darkness, exquisite and explicit.

I can see his struggle between gratitude and uneasiness. He is buffeted by all things new and strange. He does not know where he is from, who he is or what happened to him. He does not know me. There has not been enough time to transition between strangers and friendship.

This isolation of his is something I can identify with, but it is also a feeling no one can help him with until or unless he gets his own life back. And his memory.

If that doesn't happen, then it will take time for him to build a new life. He is polite to me, even friendly, but even a night together during a storm with his arms wrapped tight around my waist doesn't calm the surge I see inside him, the emptiness, the loss, possibly even panic. That night may have reinforced some trust in me, but so far not enough for him to completely relax.

He seeks me out, though. That's something. He sits by me at dinner when he can have any seat of his choosing. I watch him closely when he does not realize it. At dinner the following night after we had only 'slept' together, and before we go to bed again in separate rooms, I notice everything about him, how he moves, the way the air warms when he is closer to me, the dry sheen of his lips as they part for more air when he is reacting to something, or speaking, or eating.

His hands still shake. Anyone else might not notice because he keeps them clasped into fists at his sides or, while sitting, pressed tight to his lap.

I spend another fretful night alone. I dream restlessly, wild, loud and colorful visions I cannot recall at all as soon as my eyes open. All I know is the dreams leave me unfulfilled, impatient.

www.eyescrypublications.com

Also on Amazon or from your favorite bookseller.

SONS OF NEVERLAND
Della Van Hise

"The virtuosity shown here is only the beginning of a pyrotechnic talent unfolding into the hidden dimensions of the human and nonhuman spirit."
-Jacqueline Lichtenberg

Set against a backdrop of contemporary culture, *Sons of Neverland* explores the universal questions of love, sex and death - the three most crucial challenges every human being must face. Stefan London is a grieving man, suffering through the loss of his young daughter. When he goes to a science fiction convention in the hopes of meeting her friends, he encounters instead a young man who is dangerously seductive and undeniably magical. Lured into the night, Stefan soon discovers himself in a place where vampires are real, and the world is not at all what he has always believed, and immortality is only a deep red kiss away.

But the price of eternal life is high, and as his handsome maker warns, "Through my blood you will learn a secret which will compel you to live forever, yet a secret so sinister it will haunt you for that same eternity."

The secret will haunt you, too.

―――

"This book zones on the question of immortality. However, this is not just the decadent historical immortality of the long-lived vampire, it is immortality as a change in one's perception. This is the story behind the story, delivered by characters that are hyper-real - each one loaded with symbolism. *Sons of Neverland* will have you filled, even brimming over with the sense of Mysterium Tremendum et Fascinans. Go there for a full helping of the numinous." (A Reviewer on Amazon)

www.eyescrypublications.com
Also on Amazon or order from your favorite bookseller.

Prince of Umberlight
Alexis Fegan Black

"If Prince of Umberlight doesn't rattle your cage, you're more dead than the undead!" - **Night Readers**

Thorn may be an 800 year old vampire, but he does not possess the ability to create others of his kind, and so he is cursed to fall in love with mortals, only to watch them grow old and die. Torn by grief, Thorn denounces his immortality and enters into a comatose oblivion for decades.

When he awakens, he is no longer in London, but finds himself in a world spun into being by his own desires - a world where Time and Death do not exist, a world where it is forever autumn, where the Parish of Shadows and the River of Stars become his home. It is in this world of Umberlight that he meets Atom - an interloper into his private sanctuary, but also an impudent imp who is destined to reveal to Thorn the three dangerous elements a vampire must possess in order to become a Creator.

The Art of Brutality.
Submission to Dark Desire.
Love.

YEAR OF THE RAM
Della Van Hise

Year of the Ram was described by one reviewer as... "A space-faring male/male romance full of love, angst, and longing."

Only after Star Commander Morgan Diego becomes an exile as a result of a Galaxy Corps political blunder does he begin to realize how much he valued the companionship of his second in command - the mysterious Lucien, an Alfarian who is more elven than human, with peculiar powers & abilities which begin to unfold as he, too, realizes what he has lost.

Separated by circumstance from his former life, Morgan is thrust into a world where he must survive by his wits. When he meets a peculiar little old man calling himself Kim Le, Morgan finds himself in a situation where he is required to master The Art - not only a form of human & extraterrestrial martial arts, but a way of living and being that will alter his life forever.

At the temple, he is introduced to his new teacher, another Alfarian who begins to steal his heart - a heart which is already promised to Lucien. Torn and conflicted, Morgan struggles with the world he left behind and the world he now inhabits.

Beginning to believe he may never again return to his ship and to the friends and loved ones he left behind, he is all the more frustrated and heartbroken when a new Master arrives at the temple: a man to whom Morgan is immediately drawn both mentally and physically, a man who is strikingly familiar... yet utterly alien.

Year of the Ram is a fully-fleshed novel, approximately 97000 words, with a focus on the love story and romance angle. Set against a science fiction milieu, it explores the infinite possibilities of the human and alien heart. Sexual content is explicit, though is not the primary focus of the novel.

For those who like a romance that forces its characters to contemplate the ecstasies and the agonies of love... you will enjoy *Year of the Ram*.

www.eyescrypublications.com

Also on Amazon or order from your favorite bookseller.

All of our titles are available directly from our website, on Amazon, or may be ordered from most booksellers. Thanks for reading us!

Eye Scry Publications
A Visionary Publishing Company
www.eyescrypublications.com